MW00932004

❈   ❈   ❈

Maude clammered up the stone staircase, tripping on her robe and knocking her hat sideways. When she arrived at the top of the steps, she adjusted her wizard's hat and swept her long brown hair from her face. But, it was too late. A book fell from the pile under her arm, and Maude sadly watched it tumble all the way back down to the landing below.

Why was it always her?

❈   ❈   ❈

To Brianna~
Have fun with
Maude!
Becky Titelman

THE WONKY WITCH

by Becky Titelman

authorHOUSE™

1663 LIBERTY DRIVE, SUITE 200
BLOOMINGTON, INDIANA 47403
(800) 839-8640
WWW.AUTHORHOUSE.COM

This book is a work of fiction. People, places, events, and situations are the product of the author's imagination. Any resemblance to actual persons, living or dead, or historical events, is purely coincidental.

© 2005 Becky Titelman. All Rights Reserved.

No part of this book may be reproduced, stored in a retrieval system, or transmitted by any means without the written permission of the author.

First published by AuthorHouse 08/04/05

ISBN: 1-4208-5911-0 (sc)

Library of Congress Control Number: 2005904559

Printed in the United States of America
Bloomington, Indiana

This book is printed on acid-free paper.

✳ TABLE OF CONTENTS ✳

THE FIRST DAY, MAYBE THE LAST

The first day of school should be an exciting one, but Maude Sinks feared a disaster. Her parents had gone to this school, Abracadabra Academy, to learn more of their craft, and Maude stumbled in their footsteps. It seemed to her that she was just not meant to be a witch. The genes must have skipped over her, she thought, because they landed doubly on her younger brother. Her parents were so proud of him, and he wasn't even six years old yet. Mickey could do so many things she couldn't. He could make things in the room fly, bring things he needed to his side, and pull items out of his hat whenever he felt like it.

Maude, on the other hand, was always messing things up. She would try to do the things her brother did, but she always ended up bringing a cat to her desk instead of a pencil, making a Hiccupping Potion instead of breakfast, or pulling a pot of water out of her bag instead of her school books. Things never went her way, and she dreaded meeting other kids in school and being made fun of.

Maude had long brown hair, that was usually tied back in a braid, or two. She had rosy cheeks, a few freckles, and curious brown eyes that sparkled when she was happy. She was ten, though not very tall for her age. Mickey was five, and they had no other siblings, so, she was forced to endure his praise and listen to her wrongs, with no other confidant in the house. Maude loved to read, wished she owned a broom, and had dreamed about going away for school since she was seven. She hoped that she would do well, for her parents' sake, and maybe be able to perform a spell properly when she finished studying there.

The day before classes began, Maude had walked about the academy's grounds, by herself, seeing the castle for all that it was. It was enormous, and parts of it were creepy. She had looked at all the lawns and even the beautiful courtyard. The stone castle had been in existence in their world for many years. The Wizard Government had established it, and it was the most impressive school ever created in their world. Abracadabra was known as the leading school, turning out some of the most powerful witches and wizards of their time. The government leaders had the school built with a circle of trees surrounding its tall walls, as if the Windy Willows and Prosperous Pines would protect the students.

The school was made of stone and looked to be centuries old. The hallways inside contained statues of great wizards and were lit by Ever-Burning Candles, that were nestled in their holders along the walls and hanging in the chandeliers. Maude had glanced around the cob-webbed library, stacked with so many books and manuscripts, and she became scared of all of the knowledge she would have to absorb. She had visited the dining hall, with its brightly lit tables, many benches and chairs for the students, and another large table on a stone stage in the front. That table, Maude supposed, was for special guests.

The dorm rooms, like the one that Maude was assigned to, held five students each. The students spent eight years in the academy, and each floor was designated for that level of students. For example, the first floor contained the first years. Maude's roommates seemed nice, but Zoey, Turtain, Margit, and Plaka were lifetime friends and knew each other very well. They spent their first night out of the dorm, leaving Maude to herself. She was used to being alone, knowing that her clumsy feet and stammering tongue made kids shy away from her.

The students enrolled in this school were expected to wear the required uniform, which was complete with black boots and dark colored socks, a button-down shirt, deep colored robes, which designated their class color, and were topped off with a black pointed wizard's hat. Maude had tried on her robes and hat the night before classes began, and she found her shirt was tight at the collar, her hat too big, her deep purple robes were wrinkled, and her boots pinched her toes. She glanced at herself in front of the dingy mirror in her room and immediately took them off, ashamed of how she would appear the following day.

Maude sighed and stepped into her first class the next day. She had spent the previous night getting ready and cramming in some reading from the first chapter of every text book she had. Her tired eyes surely gave her sleepiness away. After slipping into an empty desk in the back of the creepy classroom, Maude looked around at her classmates. They seemed excited and were talking and laughing amongst themselves. She glanced at all the candles, books, and other wizard artifacts that adorned the walls and squinted in the dim light to make out if the teacher was present or not.

Across the room, she recognized a fellow student, Adair Tiptoe. He was a complete idiot that had grown up on her family's street. Maude looked at the blonde headed boy and still felt embarrassed from a past incident, when they were younger. She and Adair had gotten into a tiff over a small child's cauldron, and when they began to wrestle, Mickey had stepped in. He was all of three at the time, but her brother was quiet and strong. Adair had tumbled down a hill, due to Mickey's push. Maude had to endure the ridicule of the neighborhood kids, because her little brother had won a fight for his much older sister.

Maude knew beforehand that he would be attending this school and had been hoping he wouldn't be in any of her classes. That was the last thing she needed, to be stuck with him on group assignments. She'd fail for sure. She glanced behind her and saw the most beautiful young witch she'd ever seen. Her hat was tilted at such an angle that one side of her face was not visible. The coal black hair, that hung down on her shoulders, shone in the candlelight. Her pale face was complete with dark eyes, light pink cheeks, and pursed lips. She looked up quickly and spied Maude staring. The girl narrowed her eyes, and Maude gasped, glancing away. A shiver went through her. Maude began to think that something was terribly wrong with the dark haired girl, as she grabbed her wand and pens from her bag.

When the teacher, Miss Monkeystrap, entered the room, Maude sat upright and opened her notebook, ready for the first notes of the day. As the teacher was writing on the blackboard, with just a wave of her wand at the piece of chalk, Maude looked back over her shoulder at the dark haired girl and noticed she was whispering to her neighbor. This girl had her hat tilted, as well, but had bright red hair with magical sparkles and was concentrating on applying her Lip Wand lipstick more than paying attention in the class. They both looked up towards Maude and smiled suspiciously at her. Maude could feel herself turning red, and she turned back around towards the board. She swallowed, realizing that now there were two of them. Maude began taking notes and prayed that she wouldn't be turned to stone just for being in class.

Halfway through Miss Monkeystrap's dramatic speech, Maude knocked a quill pen from her desk. She leaned down to retrieve it and felt eyes boring into the back of her head. With her hat slowly slipping down her forehead, she glanced up and saw that the suspicious girl was sitting back, arms folded, and her quill pen was taking notes for her. Maude sighed, knowing that the other students were more advanced, and she returned to her own dull way of note taking.

When class was over, and the hawk screeched to alert them of the time, Maude realized she had been so worried about everyone else, that she had no idea what the assignment was for that night, or what the teacher had even been talking about for the whole class period. She knew it was something about their hats, or was it something about potions? She had no clue. After gathering up her books, Maude saw the dark haired girl standing in front of her, glaring.

"Hello," she said, with a menacing sound behind her words.

"Um, hi," Maude stammered, pushing her bag farther up on her shoulder.

"My name is Sini, and I happened to notice that you don't know how to properly take notes in class. Do you need to know the spell to make your quill write for you?"

Maude crumpled her face, "You can tell me how to do that?"

Sini grinned, "Of course. Are you sure you're in the right level of classes?"

"I think so. This castle is so big, I could have been in the wrong place." The girl kept staring from behind her hat, making Maude very nervous. "Why?"

"Well, it's obvious you don't know the first thing about spells. I could tutor you, if you'd like."

"Um, okay," Maude swallowed. "I'm sorry, my name is Maude, Maude Sinks."

Maude stuck out her hand towards the girl, and her little redheaded sidekick giggled.

"I don't shake hands. I make it a point never to shake hands with witches whom I don't know. You never know what side they're on," Sini grinned, evilly. "Anyway, the spell you need is 'Minute Quillonous,' just in case you need it later today. I'm Sini Ster. Don't forget my name. You'll know it all too well later."

She flipped her long black hair and walked out of the classroom, sidekick in tow. Maude stared after her and shuddered once Sini had left the room.

✻   ✻   ✻

Lunch time finally arrived, and Maude felt overwhelmed with all of her homework. It really wasn't that much, but, for Maude, there was much to learn, absorb, and hopefully, catch-up on. While looking down at her lunch from the dining hall, Maude realized that she didn't feel quite up to eating. Even her favorite drink, Snake Bite Juice, didn't appeal to her. She swung her bag up on the table and sat down. She pulled out her Beginning Spells book and flipped to the first chapter. Had Miss Monkeystrap covered the entire first chapter? Maude had no idea.

"Hi, Maude," came a voice from above her.

Maude looked up to see the scrunched face of Adair Tiptoe.

"Oh, it's you," she said, looking back down at her book.

"Are you doing your homework already? We don't have that class again for two more days."

"Well, that's the difference between you and me, Adair. I want to do well," sighed Maude. "I have to do well."

"Well, your little brother could come help you pass your classes." Adair wiped his nose with his sleeve. Maude looked up and glared at him.

"Oh, yeah? So what if my brother's smarter than me? I don't care," she spat, and turned away from the annoying boy.

"Yes, you do. It's written all over your face."

"What are you talking about?" Maude quizzed.

"Well...now it is!" Adair pulled out his wand and whipped it through the air, shouting, "Memento Facir!"

Maude felt her face become warm, and all the children around her began to laugh. She grabbed her forehead and ran for the bathroom. In the mirror, she saw it, bigger than life. MY BROTHER'S SMART-ER THAN ME!!!! Her heart sank. Maude knew she couldn't go to class like that, so she pulled at the paper towel roll and tried to wipe it off of her forehead and cheeks. She scrubbed and rubbed, but nothing happened. With her hands clenched, she ran back to the dining hall.

Adair was sitting with a few friends, across from the table where she had been. Maude stormed over to him and jerked him away from the laughing group of kids.

"Ow! Let me go, Maude!" he squeaked.

"Not until you take this off my face!" She shoved him up against the wall, grabbing his shirt with both of her hands.

"Why should I?" Adair asked, trying to appear brave.

Maude pushed him outside the room and away from all the other children, who were enjoying this lunch time entertainment.

Maude grabbed him and got in his face, "Look, Adair. I know that we haven't been the best of friends over the years, but why would you do this to me? I have enough trouble in school all by myself. I can't do all of this stuff. I'm not like you. Are you trying to make this more difficult for me?"

"I'm sorry, Maude. I was just trying to have a little fun. Those guys kind of dared me to. I was only trying to make friends."

Maude let him go and wiped his shirt. "You mean that you were trying to impress those jerks? Why? You are who you are. You shouldn't have to pull pranks on people just to make those guys like you."

"Well, you're the only one I know here, and you don't even like me. I thought maybe you could take a joke better than some of these other kids. Everyone here is so serious."

"Adair, I do like you. You're a total klutz, but I like you, I guess. Now, will you please do the reversal spell? This is embarrassing," Maude looked over his shoulder and saw heads peeking out of the hall to get a look at her face.

"Alright. Facir Memento!" Adair said, whizzing his wand around her face. "There. I'm sorry, Maude."

"It's alright," she said, touching her forehead, as if she could still feel the words there.

"No, really. I'm sorry. I just wanted to be liked," he looked down at the floor.

"Come on. Come eat your lunch with me. That's actually a good idea. I need you to tell me what Miss Monkeystrap was talking about today," she grabbed him and tugged him back in the eating hall.

"Maude, weren't you paying attention?"

She glared back at him, "No, that weird girl with the black hair kept staring at me. She was creeping me out."

They sat down beside her books and bag she had left on the table.

"That's Sini Ster. My mother warned me about her." Adair glanced over his shoulder to where the two wicked girls were sitting.

"Why did she warn you? What did she say?" Maude picked up her Snake Bite Juice and gulped down a few swallows.

"She said that she has major issues." Adair looked around and leaned in to Maude. "Her parents aren't magical."

"What?" Maude screeched.

"Ssshhhh." Adair pulled Maude closer. "They can't do magic. Supposedly, Sini is embarrassed by them. She thinks that they are disgraces to her family, and she denies them. Sini is an experienced witch and a good one, too. She doesn't want anyone to know about her parents or they might look down on her."

Maude sat upright and looked across the room. Sini was laughing with her friends, but paused when she saw Maude looking at her. The girl squinted from under her hat, and Maude looked away, quickly.

"Maude, did you hear me?"

"Yeah, I heard you," she focused back on Adair's concerned face.

"Look, don't get near her. She's dangerous. She will do anything to keep her precious reputation. You never know what it could be."

"Whatever, Adair. I can take care of myself. I'm not scared of anyone. I need to focus on school, anyway. She is the last thing on my mind."

Maude glanced back up at Sini, and her smirk was turning more vicious by the second. While feeling a creepy shiver slide up her spine again, Maude tried to concentrate on her book and not on the witch with the tilted hat.

✳   ✳   ✳

After classes were over for the day, Maude settled in her room to go over her lessons. She had just gotten a hot mug of Wormslug, all of her books were spread out on the bed, and her roommates were gone studying and hanging out with friends. Maude had lit a few scented candles to help her relax and there was a warm glow, as their light flickered on the walls.

Maude loved her room, with its tall windows and deep purple curtains, soft small carpets that soothed her feet, and the bright fireplace that always seemed to burst with a cheery blaze when Maude woke up and then would go out when she fell asleep. The beds had tall posts, deep thick quilts with purple designs, and frilly pillow covers. Her roommates had decorated the room with posters of the latest famous witches, and Plaka and Zoey's books and bottles were scattered around the room, obviously showing the hurried frustrations of their first day.

The suite that joined the three bedrooms in Maude's dorm was decorated in light, sparkling, and dark shades of purple. Next to the door was a huge fireplace, not like the small ones in the bedrooms. The sofa was full of owl feathers and was the most comfortable couch Maude had ever sat on. There were large arm chairs, footstools, bookshelves, and cabinets. Maude felt completely at home in her dorm and didn't mind studying in there by herself.

She was staring into the fireplace across from her bed, watching the flames dance, when there was a rough knock at the door. Maude climbed over her studies to answer it. Adair was standing there, all smiles.

"What do you want?"

"Hey. Want to go to the dining hall with me?" Adair asked.

"Why? I just sat down to study, and, trust me, I need it. This has been a tough day. I don't even know what I've learned. It's all floating around my head in a big jumble."

"There's something you need to see," he said, grabbing Maude's hand and dragging her out the door.

"Alright, but this better be good."

Adair and Maude tramped down to the dining hall and peeked in the door.

"Why are we hiding?"

"Ssshhh. You'll get us in trouble. Be quiet," Adair warned, pulling her head down and peeking back around the corner.

Maude looked back into the hall and saw two people sitting there, obviously waiting for something.

"Who are those two people?"

"The ones we were talking about today. Sini's parents," smiled her friend.

"Really? Why are they here?"

"I'm not sure. I think they're waiting for her to come down. I just wanted you to see them."

"Why? It's not like they're a wizard novelty or something," sighed Maude.

They heard footsteps coming from the dorms and down the stairs, towards them.

"Hurry. Over here," Adair grabbed Maude and pulled her behind a big statue by the door of the hall.

Sini walked by them, with her hat tilted as usual, her long purple robes dragging the ground, and her hair shining in the candlelight. She picked her head up and took a large breath before entering the doorway. As she continued into the hall, Adair and Maude assumed their original position by the door. They watched as she approached her parents, looked around her, as if worried that someone might see her, and then hugged them.

"Let's listen." Adair inched closer.

"No, it's wrong."

"Look, Maude. I want to find out what's going on. If you don't, leave then." He turned back, and Maude reluctantly focused back to the family.

"How was your first day, dear?" the woman asked.

"It was fine. What are you doing here?" Sini grumbled.

"We came to see how your first day went and to let you know that we're leaving town for a day or two." The man looked down at his daughter.

"Oh, really? Where are you going? Somewhere with your group, I hope."

"Of course. They will be there," the man winked.

"Good, maybe you can learn from them. I hope they teach you all something." Sini sat on one of the dining benches.

"You know, Sini, magical powers are not the most important feature. Strong will and a cunning mind mean more," the woman said, while brushing her daughter's hair back.

"No, they don't," Sini breathed through her teeth, "and I told you not to come here unless you can act like one of us. It's embarrassing."

"Well, just so you know, we are arriving at a plan. It will soon be complete, and then we can act," the man told her.

"Good. Let me know when to begin." The girl smiled evilly.

"We will. It will probably be after our trip," the mother said.

"Excellent."

Maude leaned up to Adair, "What are they talking about? What plan?"

"How should I know?" he said, confusion spreading across his face. "Here they come. Let's go." Adair grabbed her arm, and they ran back up the stone steps to Maude's dorm, panting and stumbling the whole way.

When they finally flopped down, Maude on her bed and Adair in the chair opposite her, the two of them looked at each other.

"What was that about?"

"I have no idea, Adair, but I have a strange feeling," Maude breathed.

"I'm scared. Knowing Sini, this is no joke."

"Geez, Adair, there's nothing to be scared of. They're not magical remember? This plan can't mean anything."

"They're not," Adair panted, "but she is."

THE GIRL WITH THE TILTED HAT

The next morning, Maude arose with a nervous energy. She felt like she should be on edge and watch her every move. Maybe Sini wouldn't be in her Flying Class. Maude stepped out of the castle, and the day greeted her with a light breeze. She stumbled across the grounds to meet Adair before class began. He was standing near the big trees that circled the property belonging to the school. With broomstick in hand, Maude reached him, smiling.

"I'm a little nervous about this class. I've never flown before," she said to him.

"Never? How come?" Adair questioned her, with a surprised expression.

"Well, I have enough trouble staying upright on the ground. My parents never wanted me to fly. They don't even keep their broomsticks where Mickey and I could get to them."

Adair giggled at her confession, but stopped quickly as he sighted more classmates arriving.

"Here she comes," he glared across the lawn through the sunlight.

Maude turned around and caught sight of Sini and her sidekick gracefully sweeping across the grass, their brooms floating alongside them, without being held.

"How do they do that stuff?" Maude gaped at their cleverness, sighing in her own stupidity.

She watched as the other kids, including her roommates, followed behind them. Suddenly, their teacher, Mr. Flight, swooped down from overhead on his broom. He was a thin middle-aged man, with wispy pepper colored hair that stuck out from under his flying cap and goggles. He had a red scarf tossed around his neck and wore a flying outfit made entirely of brown bat hide, which was the most expensive material in their world and also the hardest to get. Mr. Flight's brown boots shone in the sunlight, and he smiled a bright white smile, obvious that he used Oily Overbite Tooth Wax, the newest formula by their world's greatest potion maker.

"Gather round, class! Come on! Let's begin!" he shouted, enthusiastically, and his broom swept the ground, as he dismounted.

"Wow. I want to learn how to do that," Maude whispered.

As the class surrounded the teacher, Maude and Adair got shuffled to the outside of the group. Sini glared at Maude, and her sidekick shoved Adair out of the way.

"Why do they feel the need to be so rude? It's the first class of the day," Adair winced, as he rubbed his arm. The teacher didn't even seem to notice.

Mr. Flight rambled for a while about math and the physics of flying, and Maude zoned out, looking over to Sini and studying her movements and expressions.

"Now, let's put it to the test. Grab your brooms and mount them," Mr. Flight instructed.

Adair struggled to get the broom between his legs amongst the layers of his robe. Maude nervously climbed onto her broom, all the while watching the grace of Sini's mount.

"Now, rise lightly, form a line and circle the lawn. Once you have done that, land carefully. Take caution, kids. Now, begin!" Mr. Flight said and pulled down his goggles, ready to take to the air with his students.

Maude kicked the ground and her broom took off, quickly into the air. She gripped the handle and focused on not falling. But, she soon slipped around and was hanging upside down on her broom, legs wrapped around the stick and her sweaty hands losing grip.

"Adair! Help me!" she yelled.

Adair flew over to her, "Um, Maude? You're supposed to fly on the other side of the broomstick." He giggled at her frustration.

"Yeah, I know. Very funny. Now, help me, would you?"

He pulled on her robe and righted her on the proper side of her broom. She gripped the handle, adjusted her hat, and breathed a sigh of relief.

"Thanks. I could have broken my neck."

"Oh, I could have helped you with that. I know the spell to fix broken bones," he smiled.

"Shut up," Maude said, and she sped forward on her broomstick to follow the group.

She spent the rest of the class period trying to feel at ease on her broom. It felt shaky under her sweaty palms, and she clung to the handle with all of her might. Adair flew close by, to keep an eye out for any more of Maude's flying acrobatics.

Maude was just beginning to get the hang of the basics, when the teacher announced the end of class. She pulled her hat into place and squinted her eyes, determined to make a good landing. As she pushed her broom handle down and her whole body tilted towards the grass way below, Maude began her descent to where all the others were landing.

Adair came down and, after dismounting, looked around for Maude. When he glimpsed up into the sunshine, he saw her tumbling for the ground, screaming.

"Maude!" Adair yelped, jumping back on his broomstick and racing into the air.

She was falling steadily, and he stretched out both arms to grab onto her. He caught her cloak and one of her hands. Maude dangled, watching her broomstick flop onto the grass below.

"Thanks, Adair. I was almost a pancake." She swung up onto his broom and wrapped her hands around his waist, as they slowly floated down.

"What happened? You were doing so good. I thought you were looking almost as good as a pro."

"Pro? Whatever, Adair. It was the landing that gave me trouble. I think I tilted the broom too much. I slid right off the end," breathed Maude, relieved that he had come to the rescue again.

"I guess I have to watch you every class. I think I remember the spell for broken bones, but I don't like to use it. It's really long, and sometimes I mess up a few words here and there," Adair admitted.

"Oh, great. I'll remember never to break a bone, then," Maude said, while dismounting his broom.

In the dining hall that lunch hour, she nursed her arm and iced her bruises.

"This flying thing is hard. How come you're so good at it?" she complained to Adair.

"I'm not that good. I've only been flying for a little while. My parents bought me a broom for my birthday," he explained, in between gulps of Snake Bite Juice.

"I wish mine would have, then I wouldn't be such an amateur. Isn't there anything at this school I'll be good at?"

"Oh, lay off yourself, Maude. You must be strong at something. What do you like to do?" Adair wondered.

"Well, I like spells and potions. But, none of mine ever amount to what they're supposed to. I always mess something up. My mom took all my spell books away. She was afraid that I would blow up my brother."

Adair laughed, "Now that would be interesting."

"No, I'm serious," she sighed. "Well, we have Wands One and Beginning Potions today, so maybe I'll get better. Just watch out if you sit next to me."

"Oh, shut up already, Maude." Adair tugged her off the bench and to their next class.

✳ ✳ ✳

Wands One was being taught by a skinny little man that made Maude laugh. She watched his bony hands wave the wand in class, and his fingers were as thin as the wand he was holding. His name was Professor Whiskflisk, and all the students seemed to enjoy his hearty laugh and squeaky voice. He taught them how to properly hold the wand, brush it through the air, and give commands and spells that day. Their assignment was to practice in their room that night.

Maude looked at Adair, after class, "I want to practice, but I'm scared I'll kill one of my roommates."

"I'll come over, if you want. I'll help you."

Maude smiled back at him and thought about how Adair wasn't as bad as she had once believed.

✳ ✳ ✳

In their Potions Class, Mr. Pondweed explained the necessity of precise additions of ingredients to a potion. One little extra ounce of something could create disaster and thoroughly change the intended concoction. They made a trial potion in class. It was the Plumping Potion. When someone drank it, they would fatten up like a balloon. Maude and Adair worked together, taking great care and perfect measurements. When all their ingredients were added and mixed, Maude looked at the color of their potion that was bubbling in the large beaker.

"What color did he say it was supposed to be?" she asked, peering at their final product.

"Um, dark green, I think," Adair replied as he cleaned up their work area. "Why? What color is ours?"

"It's like a midnight blue," she gulped. "Is that bad?"

"I dunno. I guess we'll find out when we drink it." Adair continued to wipe down their counter space.

"We have to drink it?!" Maude sputtered, staring back at their potion.

"I swear, Maude. Don't you ever listen to anything the teachers say?"

"Apparently not," she groaned, watching the dark liquid get deeper in color.

After the potions sat long enough and were fully mixed and ready, the teacher told them all to dig in with a spoon and try some. They would fatten up and fill out their robes, and then they were to drink the reversal potion he had already prepared, which would return them to normal.

Maude nervously picked up her spoon, dipping it into the deep liquid.

"Uugghh. I can't believe we have to do this," she moaned, holding her nose to avoid tasting it.

"Bottoms up," Adair grimaced, as he spooned it into his mouth.

They sat down their spoons and swallowed, waiting for something to happen.

"I feel strange," Adair said.

"Me, too," she added. Maude looked down at herself and saw exactly what was not supposed to happen. She was shrinking. Her feet were getting smaller, and her head felt smaller. She picked up her hands, and even they were shrinking in size. Maude looked to Adair, and his head had shrunk too small for the length of his hair. He looked like a shaggy dog covered in robes. In a few minutes, they were the size of a writing pen and were standing on their stools facing each other, in mini-robes and boots.

"Adair! What did we do?!" she shouted at him.

"I don't know! You only added a teaspoon of milk-seed, right?" he panicked.

"I thought you said a whole spoonful! So, I just grabbed a bunch in my hand! Oh, no!" Maude cried.

"I hope he has the reversal potion for this!" Adair glared at her.

The teacher came wandering over and peered down at them.

"Obviously, you two did not follow the correct ingredient list." Mr. Pondweed's voice boomed like a giant's.

"I'm sorry, sir. I guess not!" Adair yelled up to him.

"Well, I'll go look up the reversal potion for this one. Hold tight, and don't go anywhere. I might not be able to find you," he giggled a little at their misfortune.

The children in the class had all finished their reversal potions and were back to normal. They crowded around the stools, laughing at the two tiny wizards. Sini seemed bigger than life and glared down at Maude, who was shivering in her miniature boots. Adair sat down and frowned at Maude. She shrugged and put her head down. She would definitely pay for this one.

✳   ✳   ✳

Later that day, when they had returned to normal size, Maude approached Adair after their last class. He was sitting in the courtyard, and Maude was relieved that a nice fall breeze was cooling him off.

"Adair, I'm really sorry about earlier. I didn't mean to…," she began.

He stood up. "Look, Maude. It's okay. Just try not be so nervous all the time. You could be a really great witch, if you put your mind to it and paid attention more in class. For someone who wants to catch up so badly, how come you never listen to what's going on?"

Maude shrugged, "I don't know. Ever since we listened in to Sini's conversation with her parents, I've been preoccupied. I'm scared something bad will happen, and I won't be prepared."

As Adair walked with her back into the school, he put his hand on her shoulder.

"Maude, nothing's going to happen. We aren't even sure what they were talking about. It could have had to do with their family money or even a plan to get back at the Wizard Government. Who knows? But, we can't let someone like Sini disrupt our daily lives all the time. Otherwise, we'll go crazy."

"I know something's going to happen, Adair. I feel it. She's more evil than you know. I get chills whenever I talk to her, and that first day of class, she said she couldn't shake my hand because she didn't know which side I was on. Sides of what? She's got something on her mind, and her parents are involved, too. What do we do?"

"Well, silly, we can't do anything yet. Not until we have some real evidence," Adair replied, as he bumped into a very tall gentleman.

"Sorry, kid," grinned the man, guiltily, with his arm wrapped around his young daughter.

Maude took in a quick breath. It was Sini's father and Sini, herself, walking arm in arm down the corridor. As Maude grabbed Adair's elbow and pulled him behind a stone statue, she whispered, "Evidence enough for you? Why else would he be back here, but to tell her that the plan is ready? We need to find out what this plan is and quick."

"Alright, let's get to work. Should we follow them?" Adair asked, turning to look after the wicked couple disappearing down the hall.

But, Maude was way ahead of him. She was already five steps behind them.

THE PLAN AND THE SPARKLY STUFF

(hasing evil was not a usual occurrence in her life, so she felt like a wizard without a wand. Maude crept around the stone wall, her hands holding tightly onto the cool bricks. She peeked around the corner and saw Sini and her dad whispering.

"What's going on?" came a squeaky voice behind her.

"Ssshhh," Maude pushed her friend back. "Nothing yet. They're talking, and I can't hear them from here. I'm scared to get any closer, Adair. I don't want her to see us."

"Okay," breathed Adair, "just watch. Something may happen. We don't necessarily need to hear what they're saying right now."

Maude flipped her head back around and adjusted her pointed hat, leaning in to try to make out their words. Suddenly, she was able to get a clue as to what was happening. Mr. Ster handed Sini a paper. What paper, Maude had no idea.

"He just handed her something. A piece of paper. A long one. Rolled up like a scroll," Maude whispered, filling Adair in on their movements. "Now, she's smiling. Her smile creeps me out. Her father has it, too. Weird family."

Adair sighed, "Enough about their facial expressions and oddities. What's going on, now?"

Maude squinted, "He's shaking her hand. He's wishing her luck, I think....Oh, my gosh!"

"What?" Adair swallowed.

"He just disappeared! How did he do that?" Maude gasped in awe.

"Geez, Maude. Come on. Let's go. She'll be coming back this way soon." Adair grabbed her sleeve, and they headed towards the dorms, quickly and quietly.

When they reached Maude's room, Plaka, her roommate, was just leaving.

"Leaving again?" Maude smiled, wondering if they would have the room to themselves to talk about what had just happened.

"Yeah, I really need to study for our Potions quiz. All those potions are so similar. I have a lot of work to do. See you guys later," Plaka waved and disappeared down the hallway.

"Okay, so what do we know so far?" Adair flopped down with a bag of GummyGuts on the floor of Maude's room.

"Well," Maude began as she unpacked her bag, looking for a feather pen. "We know that her father handed her some kind of document, and then he disappeared, which probably means no one knew he was here. How creepy! Then, Sini smiled, tucked the rolled up paper under her robe, and that's when we left."

"So, how can we figure out what this paper has on it?" Adair munched.

"I don't know. We have to get a hold of it somehow. But, I don't want to go near that girl. How are we going to get it?" Maude wondered, looking to Adair for an answer.

"We'll figure out something," swallowed Adair. "We just have to look for the right time. Maybe in a class. She might tuck it in one of her books."

"What if she doesn't carry it with her? She might worry about losing it. We'd have to get it from her dorm. How do we get into the other rooms on our floor? We only know the spell to open our own doors," Maude realized.

"Do you know anyone who lives with her?" Adair scrunched up the empty bag and began to gulp down a bottle of Snake Bite Juice.

"Only her little sidekick, that redheaded girl. She's weird, too. But, she does have cool hair," Maude saw that Adair was glaring at her. "Sorry. Focusing."

She walked around the room, with her hands behind her back, considering a thought.

"You might want to worry about something other than her hair products. How can we get into Sini's room?" Adair asked.

"That's it!" Maude shouted, flopping down beside Adair on the purple carpeting.

"What? Her hair?"

"No, Adair. Maybe, if we can't get the paper out of her robe or from her books, we could get it by asking that redheaded girl for what she uses to make her hair so sparkly. Then, we can get into the room to pretend to borrow whatever the goop is."

"No way. I'm not asking that girl for her hair stuff. I'll look like a geek. This is your department," Adair admitted, throwing his hands up.

"You already are a geek. But, okay, okay. I'll do it," Maude said, pursing her lips. "We have to do this, Adair. I want to know what their plan is. I'm going to go nuts, if I don't know what that girl is up to."

"Me, too," nodded Adair. "As long as I don't have to go ask for sparkly hair junk."

"Shut up, already," Maude laughed and hit him with a pillow.

THE WEEKEND ADVENTURE

That weekend, the first with no homework and no responsibilities, Adair asked Maude to go into town with him. He wanted to get her mind away from Sini's plotting and having to talk to Sini's friend about her hair products. He needed new quills for class and more paper, and Maude became excited to visit the little town of Caspian, because she had never been there and wanted to see the shops.

Caspian was a nice village, and it had many stores which contained supplies for the nearby students, as well as candy shops, book stores, wand and broom stands, and toy shops. The town was nestled in the valley, just past the trees that circled the school. It was a mile's walk, and Adair and Maude decided to leave early in the day, with permission granted from Mr. Flight. He held onto their brooms for safekeeping, considering that the younger students were not allowed to fly out of school grounds, unless accompanied by a teacher. Adair wanted to walk, and Maude didn't mind, hoping the fresh air and exercise would do her good and keep her mind off of Sini for a while.

Maude dressed in her robes that morning, with an excited flurry in her stomach. She primped and then walked down the hallway towards the dining hall to meet Adair. He was standing in his purple robes, leaning against the doorway waiting for her, and greeted her with an eager expression.

"Hi," she said. "Don't you want to eat before we go?"

"Well, I thought we could grab some food in Caspian. The food there is amazing, especially in The Owl Cage. I love their Chocolate Mud Pies and their Orange Reptile Juice."

Maude agreed, as the food sounded interesting. "Alright. Sounds good. Better than the everyday stuff here."

They walked out of the front door to the castle, and the brisk wind hit their faces. Maude was happy that the weather was sunny and fine, otherwise their walk would not have been as pleasant. The trees surrounding the academy were bending in the breeze, as if they were motioning the two young wizards onward to the town. The sun tried to warm them, even though it was a crisp fall day.

"So, what kind of shops are in Caspian?" Maude asked, making sure her wizard coins were safe in the pouch tucked in her pocket.

As he walked along, Adair replied, "Well, there's The Mummy, and it has books, spell papers, and supplies. Then, there's Amazing Freaks, the animal store, which is full of rats, toads, bugs, animal food and things like that. One of my favorite stores is The Crisp Cauldron. They've got all the possible ingredients for potion making. I saw wolf brains in there once."

"Eww. Gross," Maude gulped. "Maybe we can find things for a potion to make Sini disappear."

"Maude, today is about forgetting Sini, okay?"

"Alright, alright. What else?"

"There's The Spooky Spider, and that's the toy shop. I like Haunting Hallow, too. That store is full of the newest brooms and wands. They have the most expensive brooms in there. I wish I could afford one. They're so cool," Adair dreamed.

"Why don't you splurge and get one today?"

"I shouldn't. I need to keep the allowance my parents gave me for school supplies. You never know. We may have special projects and have to buy potion ingredients or something," he sighed.

"But, I thought today was about having fun," Maude pressed on.

"Yeah, but not going overboard." Adair looked questioningly at her happy face.

"Okay, okay. How much farther do we have to go?"

They looked back at the school, which seemed so much smaller in the distance.

"Not too far," he assured her. "It's over that hill. Caspian is in the next valley."

The two friends chatted happily all the way into the town. When the grass became dirt roads, with mules pulling carts along and black cats scurrying about, Maude knew they had arrived. It was just as wonderful as she had expected. Her family's small town, Dreadsville, was nothing like this. The shops weren't as old or as elegant. The roads were full of screaming children, nervous parents, and barely a shop in sight. Her father had to get all of his replacement wands and supplies for work and home from the closest town of Wenkroy.

Adair grabbed Maude's hand and pulled her to the dingy window of The Owl Cage, "Can we get some breakfast, now? I'm starved!"

"Sure. Me, too," she added, as her stomach grumbled.

Maude followed Adair into the shop, where many wizards and witches seemed to be enjoying a hearty meal. She didn't recognize any of the food, but she loved experiencing new delicacies. So, she walked over to a table with her friend and sat down, pulling the menu up to her eyes in the dim light. When their serving witch came to the table, Adair ordered them both goblets of Orange Reptile Juice. Maude studied the menu, but became more lost, having no clue what Meat Morsels and Toad Toppers were. Adair looked at Maude's confused face and just ordered them both the Chocolate Mud Pies.

She set down the menu, "I don't know what half of this stuff is."

"I didn't either the first time I came here. But, the Mud Pies are delicious. Trust me," he glowed with anticipation of the food to come.

When their witch came back with the drinks, Maude gulped down some juice and licked her lips after a few swallows. "You were right. This juice is great. Maybe we can get them to put it onto the school menu."

"Yeah, right. But, that would be great, if they did start to serve it."

Maude looked around at the tables, walls, and decorations. Many bird cages, which were rusty and old, hung empty from the ceilings. Some were even considered antiques in their world. She smiled at the owls that sat above them, cooing in their hiding places, scared of all the wizards clanking dishes and knocking mugs together in joy. There were many witches bustling about the tables, handing food to the expectant eaters and taking orders. She heard clinking and shouting from the kitchen, which was covered by a wall, so as not to show the guests the magic at work. A few owls perched on this wall and peered over at the food, which was enticing them.

"This is a neat place. No wonder you like it so much."

"Yeah. I like it a lot. My parents always bring us here when we come to Caspian. There are a few other restaurants, but this is their favorite."

"I can see why," Maude said, as the witch set down their plates, heaped with chocolate and fudge.

"These look great," Adair grinned and dug in with his fork, while Maude looked for a place on her plate to begin.

She heaped the chocolate pie onto her fork and shoved a big bite into her mouth, chewing in sheer pleasure. After swallowing, she admitted to him, "This is the best Mud Pie I've ever had." Then she giggled. "Actually, the only Mud Pie I've ever had. But, I'm definitely telling my family about this place."

They ate and talked together, contentedly. But, Adair eventually groaned and pushed his plate aside, not able to finish it all, although he wanted to. "I can't eat another bite."

"Me, either," whined Maude, wiping her mouth. "Let's pay and go walk this off."

"Good idea," Adair agreed, pulling his money from his pocket. An owl swooped down and landed on Adair's shoulder, with the bill rolled up in its beak.

"Oh, how cute!" Maude cried, as she pulled the paper from the owl's mouth and unrolled it to see the total she owed. They dropped coins in the owl's silver pouch that hung about its neck and then put the bill back in its beak. The snowy colored owl took flight back over to their serving witch, and Adair and Maude watched her pet its head and give it a treat, as she extracted the money. Then, she sent it back up to its perch.

Maude and Adair were very full and felt as if they were waddling out of the shop. They breathed in the fresh air and began to wander down the narrow road.

"There's Haunting Hallow!" Adair pointed. "Want to go look at the brooms and wands?"

"Sure," she agreed, letting Adair take her wherever he wanted to go. Her stomach was too full to make any decisions, and she gladly followed him into the store.

This store was bright and full of young wizards, wandering around and gaping at the items for sale. Maude saw new racing brooms, hunting brooms, and even slow paced brooms for the older wizards. She was in a whole new world, considering her parents never took her to places like this, scared that she'd have wanted one and they'd have to say "no". Adair was standing in front of a new bronze stained broom, with nicely clipped straws and a shiny gripping handle. His eyes were wide, and a smile curled up his face. Maude walked over to him and looked at the broom. It surely was the nicest one she'd ever seen.

"That's the one you want, isn't it?"

"Yeah," he said dreamily. "Isn't it beautiful? I've wanted it for a year."

"Then, get it, why don't you? Spend some money on yourself. You might not have another chance to buy it," Maude added, looking at her friend's happy face.

"I shouldn't," his smile dropped. "Maybe I'll ask my parents for it for Winter Solstice. They can afford it." He took another hopeful look, but sighed and walked on.

Maude walked over to the wand section of the shop. She had never seen so many wands. They were on display in the large glass counters, and other ones hung from the ceiling above, waiting to be sold. Adair joined her, and she wondered if the wand she had bought for school was even close to being as good as the ones there on display. She pointed to a copper one, and the wizard behind the cases told her, "Ten Wizard Dollars."

"Ten?" she gulped. "That'll be *my* Solstice present, too." And with that, she walked away, feeling like the wizard was overcharging his customers.

They left the store feeling lousy and decided to head to another one, maybe a little less expensive. Adair motioned towards Glitter, the jewelry store, hoping to raise Maude's feelings.

"Are you sure you want to go in with me?"

"Sure. I don't mind," he replied, happy to oblige his friend.

They entered the store, and Maude practically gasped at all the beautiful necklaces, charms, and charm bracelets. Each one held a special power and helped the one who wore it. She wandered over to the charms and found a sparkling star shaped one that caught her eye.

The witch behind the counter, with golden teeth and bright red hair, flashed them a smile and came to the case where Maude was looking.

"What does this charm mean?" Maude pointed to the star.

"It stands for courage and bravery," the witch explained. "Do you need some of that?"

"You bet," Maude whispered, and the witch looked puzzled at her young customer.

"May I get that one, please? On a necklace?"

"Of course, dear," and the red haired witch attached the star charm to a silver rope chain, as Maude counted out the coins. Adair watched her with sharp eyes, knowing why Maude felt she needed that power around her neck.

As they stepped out the door, he turned to her and grinned, "Very smooth."

"I know what you're thinking, Adair, but I think it's pretty, too. Don't you?" she asked, holding the charm up for him to get a good look.

"Whatever," he smirked.

The two friends continued to stroll along the road, after Adair had gotten the supplies he needed from The Mummy. As the sun began to set on their day of fun, Maude sighed, dreading going back to school and dealing with all of her classes and Sini and her redheaded roommate again. Adair felt her pain, too, and wished they had more time to look around in the shops.

"Why don't we get an Eyeball Ice and head back?" Adair suggested.

"Eyeball Ice?" Maude scrunched her face.

"Well, it's blue, red, and white. There are no eyeballs in it, if that's what you're worried about."

"Oh, okay," she breathed deeply, relieved she wouldn't have to eat body parts.

They purchased the ices at the candy shop, Tempting Temptations, and began the long trek to the castle. Maude licked her ice happily, and she and Adair talked all the way home, reliving their day and discussing the things they had seen. When the school came into sight, Maude and Adair looked up at its glowing windows and stately appearance.

"This school is pretty great," he said, finishing off his flavored ice.

"Yeah," Maude agreed. "I'm glad I came, even though it's been a struggle so far."

Adair looked over at her in the darkening light, "Maude?"

Maude seemed far away, as she looked at the mighty castle, "Hmm?"

"I'm sorry I ever made fun of you to the kids in the neighborhood," he admitted, remembering their tiff as younger kids.

"It's forgotten," she smiled at him, and he beamed back at her. Good thing that it was too dark for her to see his blushed cheeks.

THE PAPER FIASCO

Later that week, Maude was sitting in her room, trying to study her Potions lesson. All of the ingredients were running together in her mind, and she
couldn't remember if the lake scum went into a Disappearing Potion or a Hovering Potion. She rubbed
her tired eyes and set down her books. Her room was
rather drafty, so she put on her night robe and decided to go down the hall to see if Adair was having any
luck studying for the Potions quiz. Maybe he could
give her some advice for organizing the ingredients in
her head.

As Maude walked briskly down the corridor, she
caught a glimpse of the redheaded girl going toward
the bathroom. Her hands became sweaty, as she
thought of having to talk to this girl. The only thing
Maude knew about her was that she followed Sini
around like a puppy dog. Maude realized that she
didn't even know the girl's name.

She followed her into the bathroom and saw that
she was standing in front of the mirror, admiring and
brushing her hair. Maude took a deep breath, knowing that this was as good a time as any to confront
the girl and possibly get to Sini's paper.

"Hi," was all that came out of Maude's mouth, as
she stood next to the sink, facing the redhead.

"Are you talking to me?" the girl sneered.

"Um, yeah. Don't you remember me? Sini offered to tutor me in class last week," Maude stammered.

"Oh, yes. The girl who can't even perform a proper Writing Spell," the redhead said and turned back to the mirror.

Maude sighed, knowing that everyone in the school considered her to be a screw-up.

"Well, I saw you walking down the hall, and I've been meaning to ask your name."

"It's Evel, Evel Pest. Why do you ask?" she smirked.

"You didn't tell me the other day, and I was just curious." Maude pretended to be interested in washing her hands, as if she had come into the bathroom for a reason.

"It's because I hang out with Sini, isn't it? Everyone wishes they were her," Evel turned to Maude, with a deep grin.

"No, I actually wanted to ask you what you do to your hair that makes it so sparkly. I think it makes you stand out." Maude was digging deeper and deeper.

Evel was very pleased to hear this, because no one really was interested in her. It was always about Sini. She raised her eyebrows and smiled, "I use toad liver oil. My father gets it from a shop near the Wizard Government building. Do you really like it?"

"Oh, yes," Maude lied. "Can I see the bottle? That way I know what to look for?"

"Why not? It's in my room. No one's there now, so I guess it's okay if you come in. Just plug your ears when I say the spell to open the door." Evel flicked her hair over her shoulder and headed for the door.

Maude breathed a sigh of relief and tagged along behind her. She was wishing that Adair was with her, but she knew that he would only cause Evel to be suspicious. She was surprised at how easy a little flattering, to a usual sidekick, was. Maude expected the conversation to have taken a lot longer and been more difficult for her to get out. But, as she trailed Evel down the hall and pretended to block her ears from hearing "Doorways Entrice," Maude thought that maybe tracking down evil was in her nature.

Maude shivered as she stepped into the suite of their dorm. It was a cold, damp room and was a shabby version of the one Maude was used to down the hall. Their windows were covered and let no light in, making the purple curtains look dark and gloomy, not like the velvety, breezy ones Maude loved to see. Their fireplace was dark and ashy, no happy pictures hung on the walls, and the bookshelves held many books that were covered in dust and cobwebs. It was a chilly place and lacked the warmth of her cheery room, that always had a fire in the fireplace and smiles that adorned the faces of its inhabitants.

When they entered the bedroom, Maude could immediately tell where Sini's side of the room was. She had pictures of herself covering all of the wall space, stacks of Wicked Witch magazines, and bottles of lotions and oils that Maude had never even heard of. The room had stone and brick walls, just like Maude's did, but the air seemed darker and the light was dimmer. It was obvious to Maude that this room was a place where evil was plotted and darkness inspired.

Evel's side was littered with make-up sponges, bottles, and tonics, and Maude could tell it was Evel's by the collection of Lip Wands, her lipstick of choice. She had beauty magazines on the table by her messy bed, and open cans of Diet Snake Bite Juice everywhere. Maude wondered how come the girls who lived here were so obsessed with appearance, yet they couldn't even keep a fresh, happy, and tidy room.

Maude's eyes searched and scanned Sini's area for the paper, but with no luck.

Evel stood in front of her bed and cleared her throat, "*MY* side of the room is over here."

The glare Maude was receiving made her heart leap, and she rushed over to look at the bottle that Evel was holding.

"Wow, this looks great," she said, holding the dingy bottle to the light, but adverting her eyes to Sini's side.

"My father only buys the best. What is it your father does?" Evel pried.

"Oh, nothing much." Maude was not paying attention.

"He doesn't work?" Evel seemed surprised and put her hand to her robe, as if she took in a quick breath.

"Oh, no, he does work. I'm sorry. This bottle. I feel as if I've seen it in a store before. Yes, he does work. For Wizards Downtown, decorating for all the festivals."

"The festivals?" Evel's face lit up. "Really? Does he help with the Bunson Beauties?"

Maude knew that every girl in their world wanted to win that beauty contest. Why would Evel Pest be any different? Everyone seemed to want to befriend her, not for a real friendship, but only when they found out where her father worked.

Maude sighed, repeating this for the nine millionth time in her life, "He works with the festivals, but has nothing to do with that contest."

Evel raced to grab her shoulders, "But, he knows people! He has an 'in' with them! Can you tell him I want to enter?"

"Look, Evel. We're too young to enter, anyway. The witches who enter have to be at least fifteen years old. We're, obviously, not quite there yet."

"But, I can look fifteen! I can put on lots of puffing powder, or...no, wait! I can add wrinkles! I know the spell for that one," Evel ranted on and was running around collecting bottles and potions from all over her side of the room. She was not even looking at Maude any longer.

Maude took this opportunity and whirled around to look for the paper. She whizzed her eyes all over Sini's belongings and finally saw it lying, tied up in a black ribbon, on top of Sini's school bag. She rushed over, shoved the paper in her robe, and turned back around to see Evel, still running around with tons of lotions in her hands.

"And, I can add more toad liver oil, because fifteen year olds have much shinier hair than we do. Then, I can wear my best pair of black boots. The tips curl up and everything. And, then...."

Maude quickly snuck out the door and closed it, praying that the age-old hinges would not give her away. She smiled, as she raced down the hall, praying that Adair was still awake.

✳   ✳   ✳

When Maude reached Adair's room, out of breath, she knocked lightly on the door. No one answered, and she was about to give up, when Adair stumbled out of the doorway, hair all askew.

"What is it, Maude? It's late, you know," he blinked in the candlelight from the hall's candelabras.

"I got it," she breathed.

"Got what?" There was a pause, then his eyes widened. "The paper?"

"Yes," she rolled her eyes.

"Oh, come in. Come in," he waved her inside. She snuck over to the little bit of light that was left in the fireplace, and they crouched down together in front of it. Their shadows bounced off the wall behind them, and the few flickers of light danced in the dusty hearth. Maude felt safe to be back with Adair and wondered if Evel had realized yet that she was gone. "Well, open it." Adair's face shone back at Maude.

Maude untied the black ribbon, and the paper unrolled itself. Both children leaned in to look at the delicate handwriting on the page.

"It's a list of ingredients. So what?" Adair sighed sleepily.

"Well, it's got to mean something. I wonder what potion it's for." Maude looked over the list. "Moosegrain, Wolfbite, CandyCain, Mugrats pellets, Monkey Mind...," she read. "What is all this?"

"Sounds like pretty wicked stuff to me," Adair commented, looking over her shoulder.

"Yeah, but what is it for? Why would her father give her a list of ingredients? That doesn't sound much like a plan to me." Maude sat back and pondered over the list.

"I don't know. I don't get it, Maude. I'm sleepy. Can we pick this up in the morning?" Adair yawned.

"You mean, you can actually go back to sleep, without knowing what this is all about?"

"Yeah. Watch me." Adair got up and stumbled to his bed. Maude groaned and headed for the door. She would just have to go look it up by herself.

✳   ✳   ✳

After getting a lantern from her room, Maude continued down the hall, list in hand, to the dark, creepy library. She hoped that no teachers would see her out this late, but many other students seemed to be up. Noises and laughter leaked out of their doors as Maude crept down the hallway.

When she reached the library and opened the heavy door, she inched inside and found the potion section to be in a small corner towards the back. She dimmed her lantern to be less suspicious, pulled it up near her eyes, and began scanning the potion section. She found a big brown volume entitled "Wolfbite" and lugged it down from the shelf. Maude heaved it and the lantern over to a desk and dropped them both, with a thud that made her cringe. She held her breath for a few moments, to see if she would be caught by a teacher. No one came, and she sighed with relief. After blowing off the dust, Maude flipped the book open and looked at the Wolfbite descriptions.

*"Wolfbite is only used in advanced potions, as it is hard to obtain. One may retrieve it late at night and must be careful when handling a fresh concoction of it. There is a well known potion containing Wolfbite, which is not often used, as it has put many wizards away for eternity, due to its evil nature. This potion is the **Wonky Wash**. It is only for advanced wizards and involves a wand, a spell, and the sucking of power from nearby witches or wizards. Not many wizards will tell all of the ingredients of this potion, as everyone is scared of its power, but a few other items in that list are Monkey Mind and CandyCain."*

Maude gasped, as she looked over from the list she held and back to the book. She pulled her hands away from the pages and sat back in disbelief. CandyCain and Monkey Mind were some of the ingredients that were listed on Sini's paper. But, was Sini going to try to steal someone's powers? And, whose powers did she want to take?

Suddenly, a hand came down upon the book she was reading, and Maude jumped, looking up in the dim light at the twinkling hair.

"Oh, Evel. It's just you. You scared me to death. I thought you were a teacher."

"You better wish I was, considering this is not yours," Evel quipped and pulled Sini's paper away from Maude.

"Evel, wait. I can explain," she began.

"No, you listen to me. I thought you were a stupid witch and only interested in my hair tonic. I let you in there and trusted that you were the dumb girl I thought you were. But, it seems to me, you are smarter than we all think. So, I will return this to Sini and won't say a word to her. She's looking for this right now."

Maude gulped, "You won't tell her that I took it?"

"No," grinned the girl. "I will slip it in one of her bags, and she will never know."

"Thanks, Evel." Then a rather serious thought passed through Maude's mind. "Why are you helping me? She's your best friend. You're not going to tell on me?"

"No, I won't. Considering, you do something for me," Evel leaned in to Maude.

"What?" Maude raised her eyebrows.

"You know that little old contest?" her eyes narrowed.

Maude breathed, "Yes."

"Get me in," Evel snarled.

THE NEW PLAN

Adair flopped down by Maude at the breakfast table the following morning. Maude was so deep in thought, she didn't even notice him.

"Okay, so what did you find out? I know you didn't go right to bed last night," Adair said, in between chomps of his BoogerBun.

"No, I didn't. So much has happened. I wish you would have come with me. It was awful," she sighed and played with her spoon.

Adair swallowed, "Well, what happened? I'm not a mind reader. Although, I can't wait until we learn the spell for that."

"First, I went to the library and discovered that those ingredients are a part of a really advanced potion that sucks a wizard's powers right out of them. Then, Evel snuck up behind me and threatened me."

"Evel? Who's Evel?" Adair questioned her, with crumbs tumbling off of his face.

"Oh, Adair. Will you pay attention? The redheaded girl's name is Evel Pest. She's as wicked as Sini. We have to watch out for her, too," Maude filled him in.

"Oh. Well, why was she threatening you?"

"Because, she let me in their room, and I stole her best friend's private stuff. She found out that my dad works for the festivals, and so she wants me to get her into the Bunson Beauty contest, in exchange for not telling Sini on me. I'm beginning to think that I should have just stayed in my room last night," moaned Maude.

"But, at least we began to find out what's going on. Maybe these clues will help us figure out what Sini's up to."

"I know, but maybe I should just keep my nose where it belongs. I didn't even get to study for the Potions quiz. I was too worried that Sini was going to burst into my room, so I hid under the covers," she admitted.

"Maude, there's nothing she can do to you here at school. What do you think she'll do if she finds out? Turn you to stone?"

"I don't know. That girl is pure evil and so is her sidekick. We just need to be careful."

"Seriously, it's good that we're trying to figure this out, Maude. What if they're plotting to suck out all of our powers? That would kill the school. Imagine how much power they'd get from the teachers alone," Adair realized.

"I know. I want to know why. Why are they going to make this potion? Remember that her parents told her that they'd tell her when to act? What if she starts today?" Maude bit nervously on her orange painted fingernails.

"Calm down. We need to get to class. You think you can handle walking, or do I need to drag you there?" Adair got up and tugged on her arm.

"I'm coming." Maude gathered up her books and cleaned her dishes with a sweep of her wand, proceeding to break the water glass. She clapped a hand to her forehead. "Today is going to be horrible."

"Come on, Maude. It's okay," giggled Adair.

✳   ✳   ✳

When Maude entered the dreaded Potions class, she slid into her seat, avoiding glancing at Evel. She pulled out her book and crammed last minute information into her head before her book disappeared, which was the teacher's way of preventing cheating. All the children gasped, as their books vanished.

"Don't worry. You'll get them back after the quiz," Mr. Pondweed smiled.

Maude leaned down to get her feather pen from her bag and caught eyes with Evel, who was looking overtop of her Magnificent Mirror, which she was using to touch up her Rosy Rouge. She was grimacing in Maude's direction, and with a quick movement, Maude sat upright, as her quiz appeared on her desk. She hated the feeling of eyes looking at the back of her head and drops of sweat beaded under her pointed hat.

The quiz was grueling, and Maude was in agony the whole time. Knowing that she had failed that one, she gathered her books up slowly after the hawk screeched and class ended. Evel approached her, and Maude dropped her newly re-instated book.

"Let your father know to tell his festival friends that my crystal hat size is a five," she smirked and brushed past Maude, with a flick of her sparkling hair.

Adair rushed up to her after the girl had gone.

"What was that all about?" He looked after Evel and not at Maude's worried face.

"I don't know what to do, Adair. There's no way I can get her into that contest. My father would kill me, if I even asked. If I don't, she'll tell Sini that I stole her paper. My first weeks here have been a disaster. I'm going to fail for sure, if I keep on like this."

"Maude, stop worrying about Sini and Evel. Besides, how would she get a hold of all of those ingredients, anyway? Didn't the book you read say that they were hard to come by?" Adair soothed her.

"Yeah, but...," and she looked up to see Mr. Pondweed sitting at his desk, dictating notes for his pen to write. "She could get them here. From the Potion teacher's cabinets! Oh, no."

Maude clammered up to the desk, with Adair in tow.

"Mr. Pondweed? Sir?" she cried.

"Ah, if it isn't my shrunken wizards," he chuckled. But, seeing Maude's face, he promptly stopped. "What can I do for you, Miss Sinks?"

"Mr. Pondweed, do you have any Wolfbite in your cabinets? Do you keep CandyCain here?"

He raised his mossy eyebrows, "My dear child, those things are dangerous. Why would I keep those here in a classroom full of children and in a school with curious young wizards running around? No, no. I have no such ingredients in my stash. Only the ones for classes and the safe ones in your books."

Maude sighed a breath of relief, "Oh, thank you, sir."

"Why do you want to know, Miss Sinks?" he questioned her.

"Oh, no reason." Maude dragged Adair from the room. "We have to get to class."

❋ ❋ ❋

Later that night, with their school books spread out on the library table, Maude and Adair were desperately trying to study. Many students were chatting and laughing, because the librarian, an old witch with long gray streaked hair, had fallen asleep at her desk. Maude groaned at their loudness and watched other classmates wander around, collect books, play wizard games, and read Wicked Witch magazine. Some were even throwing candy at each other, ducking behind bookshelves for cover. Adair seemed to be having no trouble blocking out the noise, and he was just reading and taking notes, like he was the only one there. Mr. Flight had assigned a paper on flight dynamics and physics, and Maude was in total awe of Adair's ability to comprehend and understand what any of their collected information meant.

She sighed and dropped her pen, "I cannot do this! It's impossible. Why do we have to write a paper, anyway? It won't do us any good in the air."

Adair smiled at her, "Maude, you always make everything harder than it is."

"I do not. It's hard all by itself," she moaned.

"Well, at least you're not worrying about all that stuff with Sini anymore."

"Not true, Adair. I am still worrying about that. What do you think will happen if she can't get a hold of those ingredients?"

"What do you mean?" questioned the tired boy.

"If she can't get them here at school, then she can't carry out their plan. Maybe she'll become meaner because of it."

"Oh, be quiet, Maude. If she can't get them here, then her parents will probably just get them for her," Adair added, looking up at Maude, suddenly realizing what he had just said.

Maude grew wide-eyed, "Exactly. She can still get them somehow. Adair, do you think the whole school is in danger?"

"I don't know. Don't you think that something like this will damage Sini's reputation? You know how she is about that. I'm surprised that she would even go through with all of this. Her parents must have talked her into it."

"Well, whatever their plan is, we have to think of an alternate plan," Maude chewed on her fingernails, nervously.

"Alternate plan?" Adair wondered.

"Yeah, something to stop all of this."

"Maude, we don't even know what the plan is. Maybe all they're doing is collecting these ingredients. We don't know for sure that they're actually going through with this potion."

"Don't you think it's kind of odd that those ingredients add up to make a dangerous potion? You said yourself that Sini was evil. How can you doubt this? We should be prepared for the worst." Maude shut her books and began to gather up all her papers.

"Why are you so worried? Are you thinking that they'll use the potion on you? They wouldn't get very much power from you, that's for sure."

Maude glared back at him, "Don't be worried about me. I'd only be worried about yourself. Imagine if you couldn't fly anymore or even make your bed with a wave of your wand. The little things. All I'm saying is we should protect ourselves. If you want to have your wizard brains sucked out, then forget I ever said anything." With that, Maude stomped from the library and back up the stone steps to her room. At least when she was there, she was away from stupid boys and their ideas that they were invincible.

✻   ✻   ✻

The next morning at breakfast, Adair grabbed his usual BoogerBun and found Maude seated by herself, pouring over her Potions book. He walked over to her, hesitantly, and sat his tray down beside her papers. She didn't look up at him, and he noticed her bun hadn't been touched and her favorite drink of Snake Bite Juice was still full.

"Maude," he began slowly. "Can I sit with you?"

"Do what you like," she said, flipping her hair around and tilting her hat so she couldn't see his face.

"Look, I'm sorry about last night. I guess I'm just worried about you."

"Me? What about you?"

"I'm worried that, instead of concentrating on your studies, you're concerned about saving the world from Sini. She won't hurt you, Maude. I promise."

"What? Are you going to protect me or something?" she glared. "What about our friends? Shouldn't we be concerned about them? All they did was come here to study and learn. They shouldn't be put in danger."

"That's true, Maude. Okay, okay," Adair breathed. "I'll help you. You sure can be convincing you know."

Maude smiled, "You will?"

"Yeah," he grinned back. "So, where do we start?"

"Well, we need to figure out how to stop her from getting all the ingredients. Maybe one of us could find out if they need help in the MoonMail room. Then, we could stop any packages from coming to her."

"The mail room only gets packages late at night, and we have early classes, Maude. They won't let first year students work that late, will they?"

"I don't know, but it's worth a try."

"Alright. Who's in charge of the MoonMail?"

"I think that Professor Willowbeans is. He teaches some class about the earth and the plants that grow there. Supposedly, he'll help us learn when plants and seeds are ready for potions and stuff...oh, no!" Maude had an awful thought.

"What?" Adair jumped.

"He knows about potion ingredients. What if Sini already has him on her side?"

"We'll just have to take that chance. Come on, Maude. Let's go see him now. I think I know where his classroom is." Adair grabbed her robe and tugged her off the bench. "We have twenty minutes before first class. Let's go."

"Good idea. The sooner, the better." Maude quickly grabbed her things and ran after him though the hall.

THE MOONMAIL

Maude and Adair could barely breathe when they reached Professor Willowbeans' classroom. He was, of course, on the top floor of the school, at the opposite end of the building and up another winding staircase.

"Wow," gasped Adair, "you'd think no one would want to teach up here. It would take their students half an hour just to get to class. Poor Mr. Willowbeans. I hope he isn't old. These flights must be a pain."

"He might just make himself appear up here, then he doesn't have to climb flights. He's an experienced wizard, I'm sure." Maude rolled her eyes.

"Oh, yeah. I keep forgetting that all wizards aren't as inexperienced as we are. When are we going to learn that spell? I want to just appear in places. It would make life so much easier," he exhaled.

"Oh, shut it, Adair. Come on. We came up here for a reason, remember?" breathed Maude, dragging him into the room.

There was no one in the classroom, and the two friends looked about them. There were brown parcels everywhere, on top of each other and in baskets. The windows were open, and a slight breeze blew through their hair. This room seemed to be one of the cheeriest places in the school. Even the gray stone walls had the cheery fall sunlight bouncing off of them. The bookcases and desks were full of bright books, hard bound and leather bound. Maude sighed and stepped forward.

"Well, I guess we'll have to come back."

As they turned around to leave, a small voice from behind the desk called out, "I'm here, children! What can I do for you?"

The professor popped out from behind his desk, and the two friends jumped back at the sight of him. He was a short, stumpy man, with spiky silver hair that stuck out crazily all over his head. His face was full of the wrinkles of time, yet it shone with a happy and rosy expression. He looked over his funky goggles at the kids standing before him.

"What's wrong? Lizard got your tongue?" the teacher laughed.

"Hi, Mr. Willowbeans. My name is Maude Sinks, and I'm a first year student. My friend, Adair, and I were wondering if you needed any assistance in the mail room. We both are very organized people and would love to work for you."

Adair looked over at Maude, considering organization was not in her daily routine. She nudged him with her elbow to look back at the professor.

"Well, now, first years," Mr. Willowbeans began, coming around to them from behind his desk, "I don't know. I've never had such young students want to work before. All the young kids these days want to play and hang out with their friends after school. And, of course, practice their lessons." He eyeballed them up and down, as if looking for dependability.

"Oh, sir, we want to help you. It wouldn't be any problem. We can study afterwards or before we come to work," Adair added, making their case.

"Alright," he agreed. "We can try it for a while. But, if your grades begin to slip or you aren't able to get enough rest, I will have to let you go."

Maude beamed, "Sure. No problem."

"I guess you can begin tonight. My other work-er, Gobi, will be here then, and he can show you the ropes," grinned the teacher.

"Thank you so much!" Maude caught herself, as she leaped forward to shake his hand, and she turned to grab Adair, instead. "Well, we have to get to class. See you tonight, sir?"

"Possibly. Good morning, then." The professor adjusted his goggles, walked behind his desk, and dove back underneath it.

"What a weirdo," Adair whispered, as they watched him disappear.

✳ ✳ ✳

That night, Maude could barely contain herself. She was nervous and excited about possibly finding a package for Sini in the mail room. After chang-ing and putting her older robes on, she dumped her school books on her bed. As she walked down the hall to meet Adair, she passed Evel in the hall. Evel brushed past her with a conceited air, but still did not fail to give her that scary smirk before leaving her eyesight.

"Oh, no. I forgot to write to Dad. I better do that tomorrow," Maude told herself, bumping into someone ahead of her.

"Are you talking to yourself?" Adair smiled at her and rose his eyebrows in wonder.

"Kind of."

"Nice. Now, you're definitely going bonkers."

"Shut up. I just passed Evel in the hall, and I was trying to remind myself to write to my father about that dumb contest. Don't forget, our whole plan could be ruined if she tells Sini about the paper. If Sini knew we were on her trail, that could be very bad for us...and our powers, too, I'm sure."

"That's true," Adair said, as they began to climb the huge staircase to the MoonMail room.

They huffed and puffed up the stairs and finally reached the mail room. There was a tall boy, with slicked back, dark hair and a kind face, moving all the packages around and getting them organized. They were always distributed in the morning in the dining hall. Adair cleared his throat to announce their arrival, and the boy whirled around, very startled.

"Oh! You scared me!" the boy panted, grabbing his chest.

"We're sorry," Maude said, stepping forward with her hand extended. "I'm Maude, and this is Adair. Mr. Willowbeans said we could begin work tonight."

"Yes, he told me. I'm Gobi Twerp. You're the two first years, right?" the boy smiled, and his eyes shone at them.

"Yep," Adair replied and began to wander around the room, looking at all the packages.

"Don't touch anything yet," warned Gobi. "I need to tell you about the piles and their differences. Each one is for a different year. Then, there are the boys and girls piles, and there are the stacks for the different dorms. Got it?"

"Oh, yeah. Sure," Adair said, mockingly, then turned to the new boy, a little confused. "Can you repeat that?"

Gobi walked around with Maude and Adair and slowly explained the divisions and their meanings. They began to catch on and started to help with fresh packages that had just arrived. The parcels kept appearing out of thin air into some baskets over by the desk, and, every time it happened, it made Maude jump. Especially, if she was bent over one of them collecting another package. But, she got used to it as the hour wore on.

"Don't they ever stop?" Adair grumbled after a while, his back sore and tired.

"Not really. It goes on most of the night. This is the only time parents are allowed to send packages to their children. I don't know why. Wizard Government's rules, I guess." Gobi helped Maude with a large package, as he explained.

Adair walked back to the baskets and gasped, as a package appeared with Sini's name and dorm on it.

"What's wrong?" yelped Gobi, practically dropping his half of the large package, making Maude stumble under the pressure.

"Oh, nothing," Adair stammered, as he walked past Maude purposefully showing her the package. Maude's eyes became enormous, and she and Adair silently agreed that they had to get Gobi out of the mailroom, so they could figure out if this was a dangerous box or not.

Maude asked Gobi, "Do you have an early class tomorrow?"

"Yes, unfortunately. I haven't had time tonight to study for my test in that class," he sighed, looking at all the unfinished work they had yet to do.

"Well, Gobi, we know what to do now. Why don't you go back to your room and get some studying in. We can finish here," Maude tried to convince him.

"Oh, I don't know," he began, curious if the job could be trusted to two young wizards. "I could use the time. I need to get some sleep tonight, too."

Adair raised his eyebrows at Maude, "Trust us, Gobi. We can do it. We'll finish up and then go get some sleep ourselves."

"Alright. I guess that would be okay. Plus, it will help you continue to learn, and then, I can come back in the morning and check on your progress." Gobi smiled and grabbed his hat and bag from the desk.

"Thanks. We'll make you proud," returned Adair, as he practically scooted Gobi from the room.

When they were sure he was out of sight and earshot, Maude and Adair raced over to the packages for

Sini's dorm room. They found the one they wanted, and Maude plopped down on the floor with it in her hands, cupping it like it would blow up any second.

"Do you think this is it? Could the ingredients be in here?" Adair stared at the package, nervously.

"I don't know. Do you think I can shake it?" Maude wondered.

"I guess so. It's probably been through some other rough stuff to get here."

"Alright," Maude agreed and shook the parcel lightly, careful not to damage the box. The contents crackled and sputtered, and the two friends looked up at each other.

"Okay, so this probably has the ingredients in it. What do we do now? Should we keep it from Sini?" Adair asked Maude, like she had all the answers.

"I'm not sure," she hesitated.

"All I know is, we can't be sure what's in it unless we open it. But, if we do that, then it will be obvious that it was opened. Is there a way into the box without damaging the tape?"

"No way," Maude examined the package. "This thing is taped up very well. So, what do we do now?"

Adair stood up and looked down at his friend. "Maude, you know what I say?"

"What?"

"I say we let her get the package tomorrow morning."

"Are you nuts?" Maude stood also, eyes wide. "If we let her get this box, we're letting her get away with this crazy scheme of hers."

"Well, look at it this way. If we keep the package from her, eventually her parents will know she didn't get it, and we'll get in trouble. They would know it was us. Do you really think Gobi would break the rules? If we just let her get the package, we can watch what she does when she receives it in the dining hall. It's the only way. When she opens it there, we can see what's in it and not have to open it ourselves."

"Adair, I don't know about this. I'm nervous about this getting into her hands. So, if we see her open it, and it is the ingredients for that potion, what do we do then? Are we going to try to steal them away from her?"

"Let's see what happens," Adair said calmly, trying not to create excitement. "We can figure it out in the morning. Let's put it back in the basket and then finish working. I need to go finish my assignment for Flying Class."

Maude sucked in a breath and exhaled slowly, trying to steady herself. "Okay, okay. I guess you're right. That's the only way, without getting into trouble."

She set the parcel on the pile for the proper dorm and sighed.

Adair put his hand on her shoulder, "Don't worry, Maude. It'll be alright. We'll just keep an eye on her, okay?"

"Yeah, you're right. We did what we needed to do. Now, we just have to wait until tomorrow," Maude supposed.

"Yeah. Tomorrow."

THE PACKAGE

The next morning, Maude woke up bright and early, ready to get to breakfast as quickly as she could. She dressed and gathered her books, confident that they would see Sini's ingredients emerge from the package while she opened it. When Maude entered the dining hall, she saw Adair already there, reading. His Spell book was open, and it was obvious that he was trying to get work done, but failing. Adair's eyes roamed over to the door constantly. They finally rested on Maude, as she entered, and he smiled brightly, happy to share his uneasiness with a friend.

"Hi," Maude said lightly, sitting next to him.

"Hey. Ready to see what's in the box?"

"I guess so. Let's hope it's the ingredients, so we didn't go through all of this for nothing. Then again, let's hope it's not. This is confusing," Maude rambled.

Maude opened her Spell book as well and decided that she wasn't hungry for breakfast. She looked over and noticed that Adair hadn't gotten any food either.

Just then, Sini and Evel came into the room. Maude's nervousness and excitement made her feel cold and clammy, as she watched the girls chatting easily, like it was any other morning. When most of the students had taken their places, their morning mail appeared on their tables, and they grabbed for packages, notes and letters from home, newspapers, and presents. Maude didn't get anything, as usual, but watched Sini's expression, as she discovered the parcel in front of her.

Maude nudged Adair, and he looked up.

"This is it," she whispered to him, and they both honed in on the package and its receiver.

Sini opened it, as she talked and laughed with the others at her table. Evel was watching her open the package, with a face of pure excitement.

"Look at Evel," Maude directed him. "I bet she knows what's in there, too."

"Yeah," agreed Adair, staring across to the girls' table, trying to see around the other students.

"She's pulling something out. What is it? I can't see," Maude sat up taller, trying to see around the girl opposite her.

Sure enough, Sini brought out two small bags of something that looked like grass and straw. Then, she removed a plastic beaker of black liquid and a container of pink stones.

"I bet that's the Moosegrain, Monkey Mind, and Wolfbite, and that pink stuff is probably the Candy-Cain," she breathed to Adair.

He cringed, "Okay, so now she's got all the ingredients. What do we do from here?"

Maude was silently watching Sini hold up each item for Evel to see and admire.

"I don't know."

Suddenly, Evel glanced up and saw Maude's gaping expression. She narrowed her eyes and pulled Sini's arm down, to hide the bag she was holding. Maude looked away, quickly.

"Oh, no, Adair. She just saw me looking over there," Maude whispered.

"Sini?"

"No, no. Evel saw me. Great. I bet she knows that we know. But, I guess it's alright, as long as she doesn't tell Sini that she knows that we know what she's up to. And, maybe if we pretend that we don't know what she knows that we know, we'll be okay." Maude breathed and looked at her friend.

"What??" Adair was baffled.

"Oh, never mind. Let's go to class. I need to get out of here. We have to figure out what to do now."

Adair was still watching the girls.

"Snap out of it! Come on," Maude grabbed his arm, and they hurried out of the hall.

Evel sat still and watched them leave, then calmly got up and followed them.

✳   ✳   ✳

While walking down the hallway, Maude felt a tap on her shoulder, and she turned to see a bunch of shiny hair in front of her. Evel stood there, hands on hips, trying to look as menacing as possible.

"So, you saw what Sini had in her package today," she sneered.

"Yeah, we did," Adair said toughly, crossing his arms.

"So, now, you think that you know everything that's going on. Right, you little snoop?" Evel bellowed at Maude.

"Maybe I do," Maude defended herself.

"Well, just don't worry about it. Forget it all. You might want to do that. For your own good, of course."

"What if we don't?" asked Adair.

"Just try to, and we'll all be one big happy wizard family," Evel put her arm around Maude's shoulders.

"I don't want a family like yours. Sneaky, suspicious, and evil. I'd rather have my brain washed," Maude slipped, and Evel saw her guilty expression.

The girl leaned into Maude. "Not a word. Understand me? Either of you tell anyone, and you'll wish you never did. Got me? You underestimate our power. Soon everyone will know of it. But, you don't want to go spreading something like this around. Everyone will think you've lost your mind. Don't forget that Sini doesn't know that you're a big snoop. So, keep this to yourselves. If you get in our way......well, just see that you don't." With that, Evel whirled back around and headed for the dining hall.

Once Maude was able to breathe again, she looked at Adair's pale face.

"Whoa. That girl is crazy. They both are. If Evel reacted that way, I don't even want to see Sini get mad," Adair said, plainly still in shock.

❋   ❋   ❋

"Alright, so now what do we do?" Adair asked Maude, as they were sitting around after supper that evening.

"We have to get a hold of those ingredients. We have to stop her."

"Just how do you propose that we do that?"

"I guess we need to get into her room again," Maude supposed, as she sipped a piping hot mug of Bat Bubbly.

"Yeah, right, Maude. Evel won't let you in there again. She's still mad about what happened the last time, and she thinks she has you under her control because she didn't tell Sini about it." Adair tipped his mug back.

"Well, I'd say that, too. Only, I wrote to my father this afternoon, and I should hear from him sometime soon." Maude grinned at him.

"You wrote to him about the contest?"

"Yep," she swallowed. "And, no matter what his answer is, I can use his letter as a way to get into their room. I'll need to tell Evel what he says and show her his reply."

"Good thinking," he smiled back at her.

"Do you think I should take that opportunity to grab all the ingredients? Or, just get one of them, so it messes up her ability to make the potion?"

"I don't know. Whatever you think is best. I would grab it all, but you might have trouble getting the whole package past Evel, without her getting suspicious."

"True. I can just take one bag and leave her to figure it out."

"Maude, you truly are a crafty witch," Adair beamed.

"Thanks," she replied. "I think."

THE SOPPY SEAWEED

A few weeks later, the leaves outside had finished their falling, and Maude was beginning to get anxious, not having heard from her father yet. She paced around her dorm at night, getting odd glances from her roommates, and at breakfast became irritable and lost her appetite, as each day passed with no letter. Maude could deal with not reading the response she knew her father would send, but she wanted to get the ingredients away from Sini, before it was too late. Very afraid of the happenings behind Sini's dorm door, Maude passed by it every day and sighed, hoping that her dad would finally write.

To add to her problems, Maude had begun to dread Flying Class. She was always falling, tumbling, or slipping off of her broom. It became a running joke with Plaka, her roommate, to see how long she would be able to stay on during the exercises. Maude became even more embarrassed when Plaka and Adair began timing her, starting at the beginning of class.

One morning, Maude walked across the grounds towards the dreaded lesson. She sighed and tugged her broom along, with its straws sweeping the grass. Adair sensed her frustration and walked up to her.

"Look, Maude. I know you're upset that you haven't heard from your dad yet, so Plaka and I decided that we would lay off our bets about your fall-ing. We're sorry," Adair admitted.

Maude looked around his head and saw Plaka, with eyebrows raised and an apologetic expression. "It's okay. I just wish he would write! Sini could have made ten potions by now." She hissed the last part, so only Adair could hear. "And, this class certainly doesn't help cheer me up."

Adair groaned, "Come on, Maude. You're getting better. Just have faith in yourself."

The two friends walked towards the students that sat around the lawn, waiting for the teacher to swoop down from the sky, as this was his usual entrance. Maude and Adair walked up, joining Plaka, Turtain, Margit, and Zoey. Plaka patted the grass next to her, inviting Maude and her friend to have a seat.

"Maude, are you angry?" Plaka asked.

"No, I'm over it. Plus, I was beginning to wonder, myself, how long I could stay on my broom every day," she informed them.

"Well, it's no wonder, when you're a disgrace to the name of witches," came Sini's voice from across the way. Evel giggled at her comment, while brushing toad liver oil into her sparkling hair.

Adair, Maude, and their friends turned toward her and glared.

"Nice talk," Zoey growled.

"Yeah, Sini. We could come down on you, too, but we know how sensitive you are about that subject," Maude implied Sini's non-magical parents. She was happy to see the wicked girl flinch at her come back.

Sini's tongue grew still after that, and Maude chatted happily with her friends, until Mr. Flight landed and started class. He began a new exercise that day in longer flights, and the children were to rise from the ground, fly over the circling trees, past the lakes and rivers on the other side, then swoop around and fly back. Maude thought she could do the flying over the trees and rivers, but the swooping back around was going to be the difficult part.

Adair and Maude mounted side by side, and Sini and Evel glared at them from across the lawn.

"Don't worry about her. She's just trying to make you mad. You're not a disgrace, Maude." He smiled at her, in full confidence.

"Thanks, but the more I try to convince myself that I'm cut out for all of this, the more I wonder if Sini's right."

"Maude, you're doing fine. Not everyone has strength in all their subjects. I can fly well, but can't do a potion to save my life," Adair said, convincingly.

"Yeah, but I'm falling behind in *ALL* my subjects. I wonder if I've won a new record for that."

"You're too rough on yourself, Maude. You work hard and do your best. Plus, no one can do that well if they have to worry about students plotting and wicked potions. Now, come on. Let's get these brooms in the air!" He grinned at her, and she couldn't help but smile back. He had so much confidence in her, and it made her happy that someone did.

As they lifted off the ground, Maude could see other students flying in front of them, gracefully touching the tree tops with the toes of their boots. She longed to fly with such ease, and she became determined to fulfill this exercise without a single fall. Adair rose and flew alongside her, and they brushed over the trees and headed towards the lake.

"Wow, this view is really beautiful. We never get to see it from up here," Maude admired the sun shining from the lake surface and the light breeze blowing her hair back.

"Yeah. Too bad we don't always fly over here. I'm going to go down lower towards the lake. I want to see if Turtain's story about the sea monster is right," and with that, Adair whooshed down toward the waters, and she was left alone in greater heights.

Maude wanted to see the lake closer, too. A few other classmates, including Plaka, were whizzing along the top of the lake. How they were not tumbling into the waters below, Maude had no clue.

So, in order to join them, she took a deep breath and pulled her broom down, closing her eyes and hoping not to fall off. To her amazement, she flew quickly down to meet her classmates and tugged her handle up to make herself level with Adair.

"Hey, Maude," he smiled, then did a double take. "Maude??? How did you get down here?"

"Flew, you dummy," she smiled back, excited about her first nose-dive that didn't end in a mess.

Adair was proud of her accomplishment, and they flew along together, looking into the waters for the school's sea monster. It was a known legend, yet some students believed it to be true, due to the unnatural ripples and odd shapes rising out of the water at times. Maude pulled her broom to a halt and floated in the air, pointing into the lake's depths.

"I think I see it, Adair. It might be true, after all."

Adair stopped his broom and peered down into the dark water. "I don't see anything."

As the two students looked for a sign of life, Evel and Sini swooshed past them on their broomsticks. The wind and motion they caused, and also a swift elbow jab from Sini, sent Maude whirling around. Adair gasped and tried to move over to grab her hand and help her. But, it was too late. Maude tumbled from her broom and splashed into the water, head first.

As she got over the initial shock of the cold water and squinted to open her eyes, Maude realized that the lake was not as dark as it seemed from above. The water slowly began to feel warmer, and she took in all the sights of the lake-bottom. She looked around and saw rocks, odd Flaccid Fish with colorful scales, blue and pink plants, and floating all through the water was a dark green seaweed. She grabbed a handful of the seaweed and, needing air, returned to the surface.

Adair was surprised to see his friend pop her head up from the lake, and he exclaimed, "Maude! I thought you were gone for sure. Why were you down there so long?"

"Look, I found that seaweed that Mr. Pondweed was talking about the other day," she explained, holding up the dripping plant while treading water.

"Oh, so you do listen in class," Adair quipped and grabbed her free hand. "Come on up. I've got your broom."

Once Maude had pulled herself back on her broomstick and situated her sopping wet robes, she brushed her hair out of her face and adjusted her drooping hat back on her head. She slowly began to fly back up and over the trees, with Adair at her side.

"I was beginning to wonder if you were going to come back up for air."

"What happened? I felt this wind and something hit my arm, and then I was falling."

"It was Sini and Evel," he explained. "They flew by, and I think Sini hit you on purpose. She's just mad about what you said earlier."

"I don't care about her feelings. She can be mad all she wants. I fell into the water, but didn't come up empty handed," she added, admiring the rare seaweed. "Isn't this the seaweed that he showed us in our books? The one that is practically non-existent in our world? Wait until he finds out that there's tons of it right here in the lake. He'll go nuts!"

"Maude, you're the only witch I know that would be pushed into a dark lake and come up smiling, because you found seaweed."

"Well, I guess I'm trying to lighten up a little. This Sini thing has me stressed out. When my father's letter gets here, it gets here. I can't keep worrying about it. I'm driving myself insane."

THE LETTER AND THE CAULDRON

The next morning, just as Maude was losing hope, a message arrived from her father in front of her breakfast plate. Adair looked at her excitedly, as she opened it. His reply was exactly what she thought he would say.

Dearest Maude,

I knew that as soon as your little friends discovered where I work, this would become an issue. You know that I have no control over that contest, and really have no one to even ask about entering an underage witch. I would be laughed out of my job. Unfortunately, you will have to tell your friend there is no way that I can help. I cannot risk my job or put my name on the line for you this time, my dear. But, please ensure this girl that as soon as she is of age, she may enter the contest by applying with an essay. That is all I can tell you for now.

I am happy that you are doing well in school. Keep up your hard work, and never forget that your mother and I have complete confidence that you will do your best.

All my love and good wishes,

Dad

"I knew it." Maude folded the note back up. "Now, Evel will kill me."

"Maude, there's nothing you can do. If your father can't help her, then he can't help her. She has to understand."

"Understand? No, she'll just get mad and probably turn me into a powder puff or something. I wish Dad could have come through for me, just this once. Alright, I guess I'll just have to tell her the truth. I'm bringing this as my excuse to finally get into that room," she said, holding up the letter.

✳   ✳   ✳

After classes that day, Maude walked to Evel's dorm room. She was very uneasy about delivering this bad news and prayed Sini wouldn't be there to witness. Maude rapped on the door, and no one answered. The door was slightly ajar, so she thought that someone was there. She knocked again and waited.

With no one around, she peeked into the room. Their dorm seemed so cold and dark, compared to her room and Adair's room. The door creaked on its hinges, and she flinched, as she passed through the threshold.

While she looked around for the box and tucked her father's letter into her robe, her eyes rested on a glowing object by Sini's bed. Maude walked quietly over to it, realizing it was a small cauldron, bubbling with a neon green liquid. To the side of the table, where the cauldron was, sat the empty package. She leaned down and saw that all the bags and containers of the ingredients were empty. Her eyes bulged, as she realized that the potion in front of her was one of the most dangerous things in their world.

Maude backed out of the room and pulled the door to its original cracked position, and then she tore off down the hall. She ran all the way to Adair's room and burst in, to his great surprise.

"Maude? What is it? Are you alright?" He stood up and rushed to his panting friend.

"The potion! She already made it! I saw it! What do we do now? We're in danger, Adair! We have to do something!" Maude breathed heavily and doubled over.

"Oh, no! This isn't good, Maude."

"No kidding. We have to stop her! But, how do we do it now?"

THE WONKY SOCIETY

Maude and Adair stayed up that night, trying to think of a way to stop Sini's plot. With the potion maturing in Sini's room, they had to come up with an idea to stop the beginnings of the plan. Maude paced and Adair ate, which seemed to help him think. They bounced around many thoughts, but only came to one conclusion. It was impossible.

"There's got to be a way for us to stop her, Adair."

"Maude, there isn't. We've been over this a hundred times. I still say we should tell the Head Mistress. Then, we can let the teachers worry about it."

"But, we've never even met the Head Mistress. She might think we're nuts," Maude added.

"Look, we're no match for these people. If Sini's parents are involved and that whole group of theirs, too, we'll be clobbered."

"Not if we stop this, before it gets out of hand."

"Maude, the Head Mistress got her title for a reason. She could help us. She's probably the best witch in our world. How else could she run an entire school for the teaching of our craft? We have to tell her."

"But, I don't want anyone else knowing about this. We've broken dozens of rules just to find out about this plan. We could get into trouble," she pleaded.

"We'll be in a lot more trouble if we try to get in Sini's way. Plus, these people are more powerful than us and...." Adair stopped himself and stood in wonder at his own stupidity. "They have no powers!"

"What?"

"They have no powers, Maude."

"What are you talking about?"

"Sini's parents and their group must all be powerless. They need to come here, because all the powers of so many wizards are in one place. They're hiding their potion here, because no one would know or suspect anything of a bright, first year student. And, Evel must be involved, too. I bet her parents are in the group. All these parents got together and made this whole thing up. We have to tell someone!"

"Adair, we can't. Besides, how do we know that the Head Mistress will believe us? She might think we're a couple of crazy kids and send us away."

"We have to take that chance, Maude," Adair grabbed her arm. "Don't you see? It's the only way. She'll help us. I know she will."

Maude looked at the floor and sighed, "Alright, alright. We'll tell her. I need to get some sleep. My head hurts."

"Go to sleep, then. I'll meet you in the morning." Adair gently helped his friend from the room.

Maude turned to him in the doorway. "You're really smart, Adair. You know that?"

He looked at her and smiled, "I guess so. Just don't tell anyone. We're supposed to be screw-ups, remember?"

"No, that's my department," she yawned.

❋   ❋   ❋

The next morning, Maude squinted in the sunlight and rubbed the sleep from her eyes. As she was dressing, she heard the hawk squawking loudly to wake the school's children. Then, she looked up at an unfamiliar sound. A woman's gentle voice was booming through the halls, telling everyone to come to the dining hall for a student gathering. Maude shrugged and grabbed her books for class.

When she reached the dining hall, she looked around the crowded room for Adair and found him at their usual table. Other students were entering the hall, wandering to their tables, and bustling about, like every morning at breakfast time. Some were pouring over textbooks and newspapers, others chatting and laughing with their roommates, and some were gulping juice and eating hungrily.

"What's going on?" she asked, as she sat down next to him.

"No clue," he replied.

Maude looked up to the front of the room. All of the teachers were gathered at one large table, that wasn't usually occupied. She saw Professor Willowbeans and turned to Adair.

"I bet Mr. Willowbeans was wondering where we were last night."

"Oh, yeah. I forgot all about him," Adair added, gulping his drink.

She looked back up to the teachers and noticed another table set up near it, with no one seated there.

"I wonder who that other table is for," she nudged him.

"Once again, no clue."

"I thought you were supposed to be the smart one," she quipped.

Adair grinned at her, as a beautiful lady stepped to the front of the platform and raised her hands. All eyes were on her, and the students hushed at once.

"Who is that?" Maude whispered.

"Really. Do you think I know everything?" Adair giggled.

The woman had raven dark hair, on top of which a deep purple velvet hat stood. She had sweeping robes of the same color and seemed to sparkle with a glow of pride and knowledge. Maude stared in awe of this magical woman and wondered if she, in fact, could be the one Maude knew she should talk to.

"Everyone, I am Head Mistress Avalon, and I have called you here for a good reason."

The room burst into applause, especially from the first years, who were just now getting a glimpse of this beautiful witch. The older students clapped loudly and beamed with pride, as they had known her for years, and she was their role model. The woman smiled and raised her hands to quiet the children.

"Now, I want everyone to know that we will be closely watched during the weeks following your vacation. A new society in our world has come to witness the teaching and learning we do here."

Suddenly, a side door creaked open near Mistress Avalon, and a row of wizards entered and walked to the table. They were draped in dark gray and dusty black robes and smirked down towards all of the children seated in the audience. The wizards filed into place at the big table, and Maude counted sixteen of them. A few of them had wrinkles and crusty hair. Others had dark hair hanging in front of their faces, so no one could really see their eyes. They were older, about the ages of her parents, and she wondered why there would be a society to study how young wizards at Abracadabra are taught their craft. They looked too odd to have been sent by the Wizard Government, and Adair squinted to see their faces above Turtain's head.

Maude gasped, and Adair grabbed her shoulder. "What is it, Maude?"

"Sini's parents are up there," she hissed to him. "This is the group. What are they doing here?"

Adair scanned the people on the platform, standing behind their table, and he found the familiar Ster parents and their evil smirks.

"That's them, alright. I'd know that grin anywhere," Adair shuddered.

"Do you think that Mistress Avalon has any idea?" asked Maude.

"I doubt it," he whispered. "Why would she willingly let them in, if she knew?"

"This is crazy. It's like they're taking over," Maude cringed and looked over to see Sini beaming with admiration.

Mistress Avalon stopped the applause again and said, with a wave of her hand towards the newcomers, "This is the Wonky Wizard Society. They have been traveling to study how our young wizards are being taught their craft. They've been to many other schools, but ours is their final and favorite stop."

"Final is right," muttered Maude, glaring at the society. "Doesn't anyone recognize what their name means?"

"Obviously not," Adair shrugged, trying to shake his nervousness.

Mistress Avalon continued, "So, we must make these wizards at home and show them our best manners and hospitality during these next few weeks of Winter Solstice vacation. Then, they will be making frequent visits to your dorms, activities, and classes, after the holidays. Please help me welcome them."

She began to applaud, facing the table behind her on the stage. The students stood and joined her, happily, as they had no idea. Maude refused to stand, but Adair pulled her up.

"You have to, Maude. We can't look suspicious," he begged.

"They just better know what they're up against. They're not getting in my dorm."

"Just how are you going to stop them?"

"Don't worry. Mistress Avalon will stop them. I'm going to tell her tonight."

THE SOLSTICE IN THE CASTLE

Maude made herself presentable in her room, brushing through her long brown hair and tying it back in a braid. She looked at her reflection in the dusty mirror and sighed. Not what she had hoped for, but it would have to do. As she walked down the corridor, she gathered up her courage and determination. She knew that this was right and was sure her Head Mistress wouldn't let her down.

When she arrived at the tall wooden door, near the dining hall, she took a deep breath and smoothed out her robes. Upon knocking, Maude was surprised to be greeted by a small man, who peered up at her with a puzzled expression. His skin was tinted slightly green, and his deep green eyes looked her up and down. The tiny man was dressed in an elfish sort of costume, made entirely of brown wolf fur, and he had long wooly socks and tiny slippers on his feet.

"Hello, sir," Maude said. "I need to see the Head Mistress, please."

His scratchy voice replied, "What is this about, young lady?"

"Oh, please, sir. I'll wait if she's busy. But, this is very important."

He looked at her and raised one bushy eyebrow. "I'm sorry, but you'll have to come back another time."

"But, I can't come back. She needs to know now," Maude pleaded.

"Well, I'm sorry, young lady. The Head Mistress isn't here at the moment."

"Not here? You mean, she's not in the school right now?"

"She was called to the Wizard Government's annual Winter Solstice Ball. She won't be back until after the vacation. You do know that your vacation starts after class tomorrow?"

"I did hear something about that, yes," Maude looked down in frustration, forgetting all about the holidays before her.

"So, run along, now, and come to see her when classes begin again," the small man began to close the door.

"Wait!" Maude cried, holding the door open. "Did the Wonky Society go with her?" She shuddered at the thought of those wizards loose in a Head-Mistress-free school.

"They did for a few days, but will be back soon." The green tinged man looked up at her, confused. "Why do you ask, child?"

"Oh...no reason," stammered Maude, lifting her hands from the door. "Thanks for your help, sir."

When the door shut loudly behind her, Maude walked down the hallway, disappointed. She should have been delighted at the thought of the two glorious weeks that were hers to take advantage of. But, instead, she could only think of the misery that could be brought on the school, and there would be no Head Mistress to take care of the students. Maude knew the other teachers could probably handle an emergency, but not one of this magnitude, especially if their powers were taken away before they could act.

Adair was coming out of his room and saw Maude looking very worried, with her hat crushed in her hand. "What happened?" He looked into her eyes, which had lost all their usual sparkle.

"She's not here."

"What do you mean, she's not here?"

"Mistress Avalon left for the Wizard Solstice Ball, or something," she replied.

"What? Just when we need her, she's not here? Great, just great," Adair moaned. "When will she be back?"

"Not until the end of vacation. What are we going to do, Adair?"

"We just have to wait until she gets back. We could tell another teacher, maybe."

"No. We'll just wait. I have a feeling we should watch our backs during these holidays. We need to keep an eye on Sini and Evel, whenever we see them. We have to make sure they don't begin stealing powers before the Head Mistress gets back."

"What about the society?" Adair wondered.

"They went with her to the ball, but they'll be back before she is, I think."

"Nice. The school will be swarming with wicked society members and their evil children. What a wonderful Solstice this will be!" Adair said, with wide eyes.

✳ ✳ ✳

The school was beautifully decorated for the yearly celebrations during Winter Solstice. Evergreen boughs and laurel branches adorned the hearths in the dining hall, classrooms, and the dorms. Scattered among them were Ever-Burning candles, making the rooms glow with dancing and flickering light. The fireplaces crackled and their warmth illuminated the usually gloomy castle. Feasts had been planned for the next few weeks of vacation, and Maude was excited to wear her festive hat. She wondered if Adair had one, too, because she didn't want to be the only student with a sparkling blue hat.

Maude was a little sad that she would be spending the holidays at school. She had hoped that she would be able to go home and spend time with her family, but they had made plans to go visit her relatives. The holidays were her favorite time of the year. The feasts, lights, and daily celebrations made her feel warm, even though the weather outside was chilly and windy. Her father always brought home the best gifts, food, and little candies for her and Mickey. Her mother glowed with a winter happiness, that seemed brighter than her mood the rest of the year. Chores were neglected due to the festivities, and Maude went to sleep every night, snuggled under the covers, and dreamed of the gifts and cakes she would have the next day. Since the holiday was focused mainly on children, Maude dreaded the day when she would be too old to feel the excitement she and Mickey had when running down the stairs to find what presents were by the hearth.

✳   ✳   ✳

The next afternoon, after classes ended, Adair convinced Maude to go do some last minute Winter Solstice shopping in Caspian. Maude heartily agreed and was glad to get out of the castle and away from all of her worries for a while, which were mounting slowly. She dressed, and they met at the front doors. Many other students seemed to be heading out to town, as well, and among them were Plaka and Zoey. Maude was happy to be surrounded with friends, who were laughing and talking as they all set off. She tried to join in the conversation, but her thoughts got the better of her, and she strolled behind her friends, silently.

Adair, noticing the speechlessness of his usually chatty friend, grabbed her arm and tugged her up next to him. "What's wrong, Maude? I thought you'd be happy to get out of school for a while."

"I am happy, but I have this whole society thing on my mind, too. How could Mistress Avalon leave the school right now?"

"Maude, you can't expect the Head Mistress to miss an event with the Wizard Government officials. Especially, if she goes every year. Plus, she doesn't know anything about their plan, yet. We just have to sit tight until she gets back. There's no sense in worrying yourself to death."

"But, I do, anyway," Maude looked down to her boots and kicked a stone as she walked. "What if the whole school loses their powers before she gets back?"

"Stop worrying," Adair patted her arm. "Nothing will happen. Everything will be fine, okay?"

Maude sighed and tried to calm down, yet still had fears lurking in her mind. But, as the whole group entered the bustling streets of Caspian, Maude's sadness began to dry up, and she felt the wind on her face and the smells leap into her nose. She smiled, as she remembered the last time she was there with Adair. And, as she and her friend walked arm in arm, her whole outlook brightened. Adair smiled at her, knowing that her thoughts were lighter.

Plaka and Zoey rushed off to the candy store to get presents for their younger siblings, waving goodbye to Maude and Adair. Knowing they were alone, Maude turned to him, "I'm sorry that I worry so much."

"It's okay. I'm used to you," he beamed.

"No, really. I guess I'm just scared."

"Well, I'm a little worried, too. But, let's get this off of our minds. How about going into Glitter?"

"No, I think I'd rather go look at the wands and brooms."

"Good idea. I actually need to go get my little brother, Shon, a broom repair kit. He took his first broom out the other day and crashed, practically wrapping it around a tree. Mom wrote and said he'll be in quite a state for the next week or two. He's dizzy and keeps walking into things."

"That doesn't sound good," said Maude, as they walked over to Haunting Hallow. "Doesn't she know the spell for curing dizziness?"

"Yes, but father won't let her use it. He wants Shon to learn his lesson. He's kind of reckless sometimes, and my parents spent a lot of money on that broom."

The two friends stepped into the shop and parted to hunt for their own presents. Adair found the repair kits, and Maude discovered a set of wand coverings. There were protective coverings made of Topping Tape and other colorful ones in every possible shade. She picked out a dark blue one for Mickey and happily paid for it at the counter. Her younger brother was smart, but was always leaving his wand lying around, shoving it in a bag, or drawing with it in the dirt. Maude knew her parents would be pleased, because the cover would help Mickey keep his wand intact.

Adair and Maude met at the counter and continued out of the store into the bright sunshine.

"Let's go to The Owl Cage," Adair suggested. "I feel like a Mud Pie."

Maude smiled at him, "I'd rather have an ice. I'm not too hungry right now."

"Alright. It's better for us, anyway," and Adair tugged her to Tempting Temptations.

When they entered the shop, Adair's eyes rested on all the candy in front of him. He raced over to one of the displays, and Maude followed him to see what the fuss was.

"They have new flavors of Twisted Tonics! You gotta try these, Maude," he said, while handing her the little bottles with brightly colored wrappers. "They have Eggplant and Tuna flavored ones now."

Maude scrunched up her face, "These things are supposed to be candy? They sound like the gross dinners my mom tries to make."

"No, really. They sound awful, but they're not. That's the point. Twisted Tonics are great!" Adair stood up with his hands full and headed over to another area of the shop.

Maude put the tonics back quickly, so Adair wouldn't see her, and then she walked over to join him again. He was picking out a few things for his brothers and little sisters and smiled as he righted himself, heavy from his load of goodies. "I think we can check out now. You still want an ice?"

"Yeah. I'll go get us some while you pay for all that stuff," and Maude shuffled over to the ice counter, which was surrounded by a little café area for the wizards to enjoy their purchases.

The counter was made of glass and inside were the treats wizards could order. Maude took a good look, and she saw Hair Twisting Sour, Marble Smooth Muffin, Handy Candy, and Tongue Lashing flavors of ice. The multi-colored ices were bright and looked appealing, but she just decided to order the Eyeball one she was used to. A few wizards were in line before her, so she looked around the café. The bright candlelight shone down on a painted stone floor, brightly tinted every color in the rainbow. She smiled at the happy customers sitting in different sized chairs that dotted the store and huddled around the tables. The chairs all had wire backs that swirled around in interesting directions, making designs and shapes for the wizards to lean their backs on. The message board, to see the flavors of the day, changed every few seconds, and another colorful picture with a cheerful child licking an ice would appear. The wizards behind the counter wore bright red hats and different colored aprons, and all of them seemed very happy, bustling about filling orders. Maude was just about to order, when she heard a familiar voice behind her.

"Father will be so mad when he gets back," the voice of Sini floated into Maude's ears, and she desperately tried to order and not turn to look at her. The witch behind the counter went to get her ices, and she focused back on the conversation.

"Why?" Maude recognized the voice of Evel.

"The potion won't be ready for another three weeks. He wanted to begin as soon as he got back. Now, it looks like his plans won't begin as soon as he had hoped."

"Why is that bad?"

"Evel, you can be such a dumb witch. He wanted to start while the Head Mistress was away with the Wizard Government. But, I guess we'll have to get to it when we can."

"The plan will still work, won't it? My parents are counting on it."

"Of course, it'll work. It just might be a little harder with Mistress Avalon there. But, don't worry, Evel. Everything will go fine. Father will figure out the best way."

Maude turned from the counter with the two ices in her hands and pretended to be shocked to see the two evil young witches sitting there. Sini's eyes narrowed, and the two girls began to glare at her. Maude exited the area as quickly as she could and told Adair to meet her outside.

When he came out of the store, he could tell Maude was excited about something. "What is it?" Adair asked, balancing his bags and taking his ice from her.

"Sini and Evel were sitting in there by the ice counter," she breathed and slurped her melting treat.

"They were? Did they talk to you?"

"No, they glared, as usual. But, I overheard their conversation."

"What'd they say?" he wondered, eyes wide, ready for anything.

"They were talking about the potion. Supposedly, it won't be ready for three weeks. Sini's worried about how her dad will take that news. He had planned on starting their plans right away. But, now they'll have to wait, and the Head Mistress will be back in the castle before they can begin."

Adair sighed with relief, "Then, we have nothing to worry about, Maude. Thank goodness they got a late start on making that potion."

Maude grinned at her friend, "See? I knew you were worried, too."

His face dropped, realizing his cover hadn't worked. "Yeah, I was worried. So what? I was just trying to make you feel better. Can't a guy help a friend?"

"Whatever," beamed Maude, happy that he cared about the school's safety, too.

✳   ✳   ✳

After getting all their presents and returning to the school, Maude and Adair relaxed in the suite of Maude's dorm. Adair was curled up with a book about newly discovered potions and eating a bag of GummyGuts, while Maude rested on the sofa by the fire, drinking her mug of Wormslug and watching the fire dance before her.

Sleepily, Adair sat up and rubbed his eyes. "We'd better get some sleep soon. After all, tomorrow is the big celebration, and I always wake up so early. I wonder if our presents already arrived by MoonMail."

"I wish I could spend tomorrow with my parents."

"Why aren't you?" Adair asked, crumpling up his empty bag.

"Because, they took Mickey and went to visit my great aunt Sila. She lives hours from here and is a crazy old witch. I'm actually glad that I don't have to go with them. She always pinches my cheeks and tells me what a fine witch I'm growing up to be. Do you have any relatives like her?"

"Oh, yeah," Adair laughed. "My Granny is just like that. I hate when she does that to me. My little sisters get more presents than any of the boys in my family. She always pours the money out for their presents, and they get the coolest stuff. Last year, Mikah got a new broom and a new cauldron. She's only five! Then, Terah got a potions set and a pet rabbit. I only got a bag of candy. She always gives the girls the best gifts. If she likes them so much, why does she have to pinch and kiss all over me?" Adair protested, and Maude laughed heartily.

"Old relatives can be annoying sometimes," she smiled.

"You're telling me." Adair stood up and stretched, grabbing his book.

"Why didn't *you* go home for Solstice?" Maude asked him.

"Oh, my parents figured I could use the study time, and they had a lot of planning and cooking to do before my relatives arrived. So, they couldn't drive to get me."

"That's sad."

"Yeah, but I'll live. My house is always insane over the holidays. This vacation will actually be peaceful. It'll be nice not to have to chase my four little brothers and six sisters around."

"You have ten brothers and sisters?" Maude sat upright, shocked.

"Unfortunately. Well, I better get to bed. See you in the morning."

"Yeah," Maude said, finishing off her drink. "Let's meet here. Bring your presents over, and we can open them all together. It's kind of lonely in here, since all of my roommates went home tonight."

"Alright. Good night." Adair shut the door, and Maude leaned back, relieved to be facing the holidays and not more classes.

Maude felt her heart drop slightly, though, as she fanned the fire and pulled out a book, trying to get a little ahead in Potions for the new semester. She missed her family, even if Mickey was a pain some of the time. He loved to pick fights, especially when she didn't know the proper spells to get their chores done quickly. Maude always tried to help. Once, she had turned the mop into a horse, instead of making it magically begin to slop soap and water on the floor. They spent most of their chore time trying to get the small pony out of the house, and by the time their parents came home, the horse had settled on the sofa for a nap. Mickey and Maude were a mess with their hair askew and dusty faces, and their parents were disappointed about the dirty state of the house. Mickey finally made the horse disappear, and the mop reappeared, making the couch a wet, soapy disaster. They were sent to their rooms, and Maude was upset that she couldn't perform a simple cleaning spell. Mickey was mad at her for days, since he was punished for something that wasn't his fault.

But, during the holidays, Mickey seemed to be an angel. They got along better than the rest of the year, and the siblings would talk excitedly in each other's rooms about the food, cakes, and gifts that were expected. The big celebration always was fun for Maude, with its candles, songs, games, and full stomachs. She would miss that, but hoped that Adair could bring some happiness to her vacation. Maude made up her mind to have fun, relax, and put Sini far from her thoughts, as she climbed into bed and listened to the calm silence in her room, which was usually filled with the giggles of her roommates.

✳   ✳   ✳

Maude heard Adair's happy voice first thing the next morning. She blinked in the sunlight, as he yelled for her to come into the room. She put on her night robe and stumbled out to see rows of presents for her by the warm hearth, surrounded with Ever-Burning Candles. Adair was smiling ear to ear, and Maude wished him a "Happy Solstice."

"You, too," he added, pointing to her huge pile of presents. "Looks like you were good this year."

"You seem to have a few packages there, yourself," Maude said, while sitting down on the rug to view her gifts from her family.

"Open this one first. It's from me." He handed her a bright shiny package, and she agreed, tearing open the paper. It was a book called "Flying for Dummies." Maude laughed, and Adair grinned.

"Thanks a lot, you goof," she smiled.

"I thought you'd laugh."

"Here. This one's from me," she giggled, handing him a red parcel from the pile, which also held presents for her family, a few friends who had gone away, and for some of her teachers.

Adair tore into her beautiful wrapping job and grinned, as he pulled out a coupon from the box. Maude had made the first payment for his new broom. The one he wanted so badly from Haunting Hallow. He looked up at her with a bright twinkle in his eyes, "Maude, I can't believe you did this. Are you crazy? That must have been a lot of money."

"No, it really wasn't. Now you have to come up with the rest, and then you'll have your broom."

Adair threw his arms around her neck, thanking her. "Maude, you're the best!"

"Oh, Adair, that's what friends are for."

The two young wizards continued to open gifts, the bad and the good, and fell on the sofa when all were opened. Maude stared at her piles of homemade cakes, wizard toys, brightly colored books, delicious candy, sparkling jewelry, strong incense, holiday candles, and dress robes, and she smiled at her family's thoughtfulness. Adair reveled in his stacks of crooked hats, spell books, Twisted Tonics, and Ghostly Games, but he held the coupon for his new broom still in his hand.

"Well, I guess this was a pretty good morning, after all." Maude smiled, tired from the excitement.

"Sure was," Adair added, mouth full of candy.

"I was worried about the society, Sini, and Evel ruining everything."

"I told you it would be alright. You never believe me."

"I do, too. I just don't always say it," she admitted.

"That's okay. As long as you think it," Adair smiled. "Now, let's go get some breakfast. I worked up a good appetite opening all those presents."

"Me, too. Let's eat."

The halls seemed to glow with seasonal merriment, as the two friends chatted happily while walking to the dining hall. All the candles and fireplaces were lit, and the few students that had stayed for the vacation were crowded around their breakfast tables, laughing and enjoying some of their new toys. Maude and Adair piled their plates high with the holiday goodies and sat at their usual table to dig into their feast. Adair smiled and crammed Energy Eggs into his mouth, while Maude nibbled daintily on her Tainted Tarts. In Maude's mind, nothing could ruin this holiday for her. It hadn't been so bad being away from home.

Maude was excited to finish breakfast that morning, so she could go write a long letter to her parents. Maybe she'd even write a little note to Mickey, asking him if he got everything he wanted. She'd send her presents that night and hope to receive a letter back, telling about their visits with Aunt Sila and the rest of the family.

THE HEAD MISTRESS

Maude spent the remainder of her vacation time reading, playing wizard games with Adair, taking an occasional trip to Caspian to cure boredom, and wondering what the society was up to while they flitted about the castle. She had passed Sini and Evel a few times in the corridor when they were walking around with their parents. It seemed to Maude and Adair that they had taken over the school. They were at every big meal and were constantly parading up and down the hallways, keeping an eye on all activity. But, everything had been relatively quiet, being that nothing could be done to advance their plans without the potion at its peak of maturity. Maude cowered whenever she saw them coming, even though she knew they could not harm her, and she waited patiently for the Mistress's return.

When vacation was over, Maude dropped her school books off in her room after their first classes of the new term. She splashed her face with GlowGlop and brushed back her hair. She wanted to look her best for meeting the Head Mistress and not look like a raving lunatic. She hoped a pretty appearance might soften the woman's heart and make her listen.

Maude wandered through the halls towards the dining room, as her robes swished and flowed about her ankles. When she reached the large wooden door at the end of the hall, she took a deep breath and knocked as loudly as she could. The small man opened the door and peered up at Maude.

"Hello, again, sir," Maude said. "I need to see the Head Mistress, please."

His scratchy voice replied, "She is meeting with the society right now."

"Oh, I'll wait."

"Alright. Come in. But, you'll have to wait in her study," the man said and showed Maude in.

She walked through the door and looked about. The hallways were stone, but bright. She was taken into a library sort of room and told to sit on one of the high-backed chairs. Maude felt as if she was on a throne, but sat obediently and placed her sweaty hands together in her lap.

The man left her to wait, and she nervously glanced around the study. There were many books and witch artifacts surrounding the walls. The shelves were full of novels and hardbound books. Maude noticed one of her favorites, "The Tiger, the Witch, and the Cupboard." She smiled and sighed, continuing to glance around. There were glass cases filled with skulls, candles, old bones, and small stuffed bats. The bats looked wicked to Maude, and she shuddered while staring at their bared teeth.

Suddenly, the man re-entered and spoke, "Mistress Avalon will see you now."

Maude practically jumped up, and she followed him down the hallway to another larger room with two big staircases in it.

"Sit, and she'll be right in." The man bowed and left Maude again, by herself.

She took a place in a chair that faced the large wooden desk. The desk had papers, books, and maps scattered about on it and a big inkstand with a few feather quill pens sticking out. Maude looked out the windows, to her left, and noticed that the sun had completely set. She wondered what Adair was up to, as her feet twitched nervously underneath her.

"Hello, my young student. What can I do for you, today?"

Maude looked up to see that Mistress Avalon was coming down one of the staircases, books in hand. She spoke as if she saw Maude every day.

"Yes, ma'am. My name is Maude. Maude Sinks."

"Nice to meet you, Miss Sinks. How can I help you?" Mistress Avalon asked sweetly, while sitting down at her desk and facing Maude.

"Well, ma'am. I'm not sure where to start."

"At the beginning would be best, I suppose," the woman smiled.

Maude cleared her throat and began to tell her story. Mistress Avalon watched and listened with total concentration and a sad, furrowed look came over her face. Maude was beginning to wonder if she should have even come at all, when Mistress Avalon rose from her chair and began to pace the floor. The storyteller watched her walk back and forth, as the tale evolved and was absorbed. When Maude finally finished, Mistress Avalon sat back down and leaned in, hands crossed.

"So, what you're telling me, Miss Sinks, is that this nice society I have chatted with all afternoon is really plotting to take over the powers of my entire school?" she questioned the young witch.

"Yes, ma'am. I know it all seems crazy, but I kind of stumbled upon it. I had to wait these last two weeks of vacation to tell you, since you were away. But, I wanted you to know. You should know before anyone else."

"Does anyone else here know about this, at all?"

"Only my best friend, Adair. He's a first year, too."

Mistress Avalon left her chair again, walked over to Maude, and sat down on the edge of her desk, looking seriously at her young student.

"Dear, are you sure you are correct on all of this? I can't go blaming a group of wizards if your facts are not correct."

"Oh, yes, ma'am. I wouldn't waste your time if it wasn't true. I just didn't know who else to tell."

The Head Mistress rose and stood above the girl. "Well, my dear. You came to the right person. Do you have any concrete proof of all of this?"

"No, ma'am. Evel took the ingredient list from me. I'm sorry," Maude bowed her head.

"What I need for you to do, young lady, is bring me proof. This group seemed genuine to me, so you need to prove me wrong."

"Wrong? Prove *you* wrong, ma'am?"

"Yes. You want me to help, and I shall. But, only if you can show me that I should believe you. I want to, but I must do what's best for the whole school. Understand?"

"Yes, ma'am. I'll try," Maude agreed and shook the Mistress's hand. "Thank you."

As the wooden door shut behind Maude, she took a deep breath and leaned against it. How was she going to get that list, now? Maude thought hard, and, suddenly, it came to her. She had tried to use the letter before, but no one had been in the room. The letter from her father would get her into Sini and Evel's dorm this time. She raced down the hall to find Adair.

THE TASK

Maude told Adair all about her meeting with the Head Mistress. He was sad that he didn't go, when Maude informed him of all the neat artifacts and books that were in her rooms. He also wished that he could have met the green man.

"Oh, Adair, you don't even care about the meeting. You just wanted to go to see all the stuff she has in there. She's going to help us. Did you miss that part of the story?"

"No, but we have to get the list first. I want to know how you think you're going to do that, now that Evel's onto us."

"Well, the last time I tried to get into Sini's room, there was no one there. I still haven't told Evel about the letter from my dad. She needs to know that he can't get her into that contest. That's how I'll get in there again and deliver the bad news, too," Maude sighed and sat down. "Although, I have to admit that I'm not looking forward to it."

"I wouldn't either," Adair agreed. "But, maybe you can sneak a look at the potion while you're there. Did the book you read say what color it has to turn before it's ready?"

"No, I didn't read that far. Evel came in and scared the life out of me, so I just stopped reading and got out of there."

"I don't blame you." Adair walked over to her. "So, when are you going?"

✳   ✳   ✳

Maude walked down the hallway, trying to seem at ease. She felt for the letter in her robes and made sure that it was secure in her inner pocket. After a few deep breaths, she knocked on the door and waited. Evel answered, with her hair shining even more than usual, and she raised her eyebrows.

"What do you want, snoopy?"

Maude gulped, "Well, I wrote to my father, and I have his reply." She held up the letter.

Evel grabbed Maude's robe and tugged her into the room, shutting the door. Maude looked over to the neon yellow, bubbling potion, and Evel grabbed her and spun her back around.

"Don't even think about it," she hissed. "So? Can I see this letter?"

"It's not good news, I'm afraid," Maude warned her.

"What do you mean? I told you to get me in. This is not an option," Evel growled.

"Evel, I have no control over this. If he can't do it, he can't do it."

"Well, then *I'll* write to him. I'll let him know what you've been up to and that you promised you'd get me into the contest."

Maude froze, "Don't do that, Evel. Let me try, again. Maybe I can convince him. But, I need something from you, first."

"What? Your life is being saved right now, because I'm not telling Sini. Don't you think that's enough?" the girl glared at her.

"No, I don't," Maude tried to sound firm. "I need that old list of Sini's."

"Are you kidding? Why would you need that?"

"Well, you all obviously don't need it anymore," she motioned to the cauldron. "I want to write a paper on that potion for class. I thought maybe you could help me, considering that the books don't say what all of the ingredients are."

"Help you?" Evel laughed and walked over to the cauldron. "Why should I help you?"

"I guess you could help me because I haven't gone to anyone about all this. I have saved you and Sini from getting expelled and in even bigger trouble with the Wizard Government. No list, and I tell." Maude stood hands on hips, tired of the threats and ready to take action. "Plus, I'll write again to my dad. Need any more reasons?"

Evel stared her down, "Alright. The list is over there on that table. I better figure out how to tell Sini that it's gone."

"Tell her you threw it away or something. Plus, if it fell into the wrong hands, people might suspect what you're up to. You shouldn't let something like this lie around. The two of you should have gotten rid of it right after you made the potion. But, what do I know? I'm just a stupid snoop, right?" Maude seethed, as she grabbed the paper and left the room, proud of how she stood up to Evel.

Although, as she walked down the hall with the list in her hand, she became more doubtful. Sini and Evel were more powerful than her and could sneak up on her at anytime. She was worried about threatening Evel. Maybe that wasn't the right path to take, however, Evel had seemed more concerned about the contest. Maude took a deep breath and tried to not worry. But, a vision of Sini sucking out her powers stayed with her the rest of the night, and she tossed and turned until the sun rose on another day.

THE MISTRESS'S PROMISE

Adair met Maude with a face full of concern the next morning. He could barely contain himself, as she sat down next to him at breakfast.

"So? Did you get the list?" he wondered, sitting as still as he could.

"Yeah. I got it, alright."

"Then, why do you look so upset? This thing will be over soon, once you take it to Mistress Avalon."

"Don't be sure about that," grumbled Maude, irritable from lack of sleep.

"What's wrong with you?" he quizzed.

"Well, I got the list from Evel by threatening her that we'd tell about the potion if she didn't give it to me. I told her that they should have destroyed it, because anyone could find it if they left it out like that. I also told her that I needed it for a writing assignment about the potion for a class. Adair, she's in all of our classes. The dummy didn't even realize that we have no paper due. All she cares about is that stupid contest, which I have to write to my dad about, again."

"Why?"

"Because, I told her I would," Maude sighed. "It helped me get the list."

"But, once you show the Head Mistress the paper, which is your proof about the plot, they'll both be in so much trouble that the contest will be the farthest thing from their minds," Adair added.

"I guess that's true."

"Don't worry about the contest and the letter. Go see Mistress Avalon. With her on our side, we can fight back. She'll know what to do about all of this."

"Alright, we have a few minutes before class. Should we go now?"

"Can I come this time?" Adair grinned, glad to help.

"Sure. Let's go."

✳　　　✳　　　✳

When Maude and Adair sat in the chairs opposite the Mistress's desk, they stared around and twiddled their hands in their laps. Just being in there made them both feel nervous, and they could feel how powerful the one who walked these floors was. Adair looked over at his friend, and he smiled, sweetly.

"Don't worry, Maude. You have your evidence. Just relax."

"I know, but it's still a serious thing. This could change the school as we know it."

"So could they, if we let them get away with this plan of theirs. Then a good deal of the young wizards in our world will have no powers. Let's just see what she has to say about it," and Adair focused his attention to the Mistress, as she entered from above them on the staircase.

"Well, hello again, Miss Sinks," she said happily, descending the stairs. "Who is this with you?"

Maude and Adair stood up, "This is my friend I told you about. The only other student who knows about the plot. His name is Adair Tiptoe."

"Nice to meet you, young man," the Mistress added, shaking his hand lightly.

"You too, Head Mistress Avalon," Adair smiled.

"What brings you back again, dear?" she turned back to Maude.

"You told me to come back with my evidence."

"Ah, yes. And?"

"Here it is," Maude whipped out the paper from her robes.

Mistress Avalon scanned the list, while her face slowly sunk in despair.

"Yes, this is it," she sighed. "The Wonky Wash. I had hoped you had been lying to me. I can't believe that the society and a few students would try to kill the powers in my whole school. This is just so sad."

"We know," Adair added. "We've been trying to make sure that they were actually going through with all of this, before going to anyone. Once we saw the society here at the school and their name being the 'Wonky' society, we knew that we had to do something. We couldn't believe that you didn't see it in their name alone."

"I just overlooked it, I guess," said the woman sadly. "I never trust names. We have many odd names in our world. I suppose I thought it was a coincidence."

"So, what do we do now, Mistress Avalon?" Maude asked.

"Yeah," Adair said.

"Well, children, it is up to me, now. I must take on the society and ask them to leave."

"Ask them? They're plotting to take over the school's powers, and you're just going to ASK them to leave? What about Sini and Evel? The potion's in their dorm room!" Maude questioned her, very flustered.

The Head Mistress smiled, "Calm down, child. I know what I'm doing. Trust me, no harm will come to you two. Or the rest of the school, for that matter. I promise you."

Maude sighed and sat back. She knew she should trust Mistress Avalon, but she was scared that the potion was going to be ready very soon and the plan underway, and then no one could stop it. The society's powers would be too great, then. Adair glanced at her, nervously, as they watched the Mistress pace around the room.

"I thought you said she'd help. I'm scared she doesn't know what to do," whispered Adair.

"She knows, alright. She just won't tell us. She doesn't have to. It's in her hands, now." Maude had noticed the glimmer in her Head Mistress's eyes and the sparkle of a plan forming. She had full confidence that this woman knew exactly what to do.

THE WONKY WASH AND THE CLOSET

As Maude went back to her room, exhausted from her meeting with the Head Mistress and her classes, she passed by Sini's dorm. While walking by, she heard loud voices and bickering behind the door. Maude looked up and down the hall, to be sure she was alone. With no one around, she leaned her ear to the wooden door and heard the voices of Sini, Sini's father, and Evel.

"Father, we can't! Not yet! The potion won't be ready until two days from now. If we start tonight, it could all go wrong! It might not even work the way we want it to," yelled Sini.

"Look, we've waited long enough. The Head Mistress was looking at us strangely today, and I think she may be catching on. We must act!" the man's voice grumbled.

"We shouldn't, sir," came Evel's voice. "What if something goes wrong? We could all be imprisoned or worse."

"I know what I'm doing, children. Now, give me that potion!" her father growled.

"No! I won't let you! You can wait, Dad. I know it will be better if we do," Sini said, desperately.

"It must begin tonight. You both know what to do."

With that, Maude ran down the hall to find Adair, praying that he was in his dorm room and that she wouldn't have to search the whole castle for him. Luckily, he opened the door when she knocked.

"Thank goodness, Adair!" she exclaimed, grabbing him by the shirt and pulling him into the hall.

"What is it?" he wondered, totally confused.

"They're beginning the plan right now. As we speak, even. We have to go tell the Head Mistress," Maude breathed.

"How do you know?"

"I just over heard them. I was walking back to my room after class and heard Sini, Evel, and Sini's father yelling at each other. So, I listened at the door," she explained, pulling him from the doorway. "We have to go, now!"

"Alright, alright. Let's go." Adair pulled his door shut and followed his running friend down the hall.

As they passed Sini's dorm on the way, Sini, herself, and Evel stepped out of their room. By the looks on Maude and Adair's faces, Evel knew that they had a clue.

"Where are you two going?" Sini grinned.

"Probably to study, so the two snoops don't fail." Evel looked right at Maude.

Maude's face dropped. Sini knew, and Evel had told her.

"I hope that you weren't coming to see if we were out of our room. That wouldn't be a good idea. Especially now," seethed Sini.

"Oh, now that you plan to destroy our school and all of our powers?" Maude glared at her.

"This is ridiculous," Sini sighed. "I don't need to explain myself to you."

"The students here work to get power, right? To ensure they know everything they need to know, before going off into our world," stepped in Evel.

"Right. What's your point?" Maude was very confused.

"That's what we are doing. Getting the power we deserve," Sini explained.

"But, it's not for you, it's for your parents," Adair replied.

"Some will go to the parents who have no powers, and some will transfer to us. We will become stronger," Evel glared at them.

"Oh, I understand. The only reason you agreed to help your parents become more powerful and not disgrace you anymore, is that you'll get more power, as well. I get it," Maude nodded, still glaring. "So, you'll risk the lives of everyone in school for it?"

"I don't care about them," Sini sneered.

"That's obvious," quipped Adair.

"Come on, Evel. They know too much," Sini said, grabbing Adair by the collars, and tugging him in their room. Evel got a hold of Maude before she could fight back, and the two friends were dragged into the dorm and shoved in a dark closet.

As Maude bumped against the back wall and got twisted in the clothes, she said, "What do we do now, Adair? We need to get to the Head Mistress!"

"I don't know. We have to get out of here," he scrambled for the door handle.

Just then, they heard a spell cast on the door.

"Lockunous Immediatude!" they heard Sini shout, and then the door to the dorm room slammed. The only sounds the two could hear were the gurgling potion and the steps of the running girls fading down the hallway.

"Now, what do we do?" Adair groaned. "It's hot in here."

"Forget that," grumbled Maude, right back to him. "We have to get out. Do you know the reversal spell for the one she just did?"

"No, I wish I did. Then, we could just get the potion and dump it out the window, so all of this could be over," Adair sighed, feeling for a place to sit in the darkness.

"Where are you?" Maude asked, trying to sit down amongst the shoes, boxes, laundry, and books that lined the bottom of the closet.

"Right here. I'm sitting next to you."

"Okay." Maude felt less nervous with Adair by her side. "I don't know what we're going to do, now."

"Well, let's think," Adair began. "One of us has to know a spell to get us out of here."

"Not me," admitted Maude. "I have trouble with spells, remember?"

"Yeah, I know. But, there's got to be some spell we're not thinking of."

"Like what?"

"I don't know. One that we never expected to use when sitting in a closet while two evil girls and a society proceed with a wicked plot," Adair added.

Maude looked over to Adair's faint outline across from her. "I'm sorry, Adair."

"What for?" he questioned.

"For getting us into this mess. I never should have started snooping in the first place."

"But, think where we would be if you hadn't. The whole school would be in danger."

"It still is in danger. We need the Head Mistress's help."

"Yeah, but she'll never know we're in here. How can we get someone's attention?" added Adair, feeling the walls and the door for a crack or loose board.

"No one could ever hear us all the way in here," Maude complained. "I wonder if there's something in here we can use to escape."

Maude reached inside of her robes, feeling stupid for not thinking of it before, and pulled out her wand. She said the spell that lit up her wand like a flashlight, and its brightness bounced off of the small closet walls. Adair winced in the new light and covered his eyes with his arm.

"Maude, shine it the other way. I don't want to go blind."

"Oh sorry," she said and pulled the light towards the back of the closet, resting on some books.

"Wow. Look at these titles! These are definitely advanced magic books. We don't take these classes until seventh year," Maude informed him.

"Are there any spell books there?"

"I don't know. Why?" she wondered.

"Because, Maude, the reversal spell could be in one of those books. We're trying to find a way out, remember?" Adair rolled his eyes.

"I know that. Hold this," she handed him her wand and began to thoroughly search the titles. "Here's one!"

Maude slid the dusty volume out from the stack and began flipping through the pages.

"Lizards, Limping, Lumpiness.....it's not here! How can the reversal spell for locks not be in here?" she groaned, tossing the book aside.

"Maude, calm down. If it's not in there, it's probably because it has more advanced spells in it. Maybe locks were covered in an earlier volume. Let's see if there's anything we *can* use in there." Adair picked up the book and flipped to the table of contents. "Okay, well, there's a chapter on how to turn objects into other things."

"We don't need that one. Next," Maude said in frustration.

"Yes, this is it!"

"What's it?" she looked to Adair for an explanation.

"We can turn the closet into something else!" he beamed.

"Oh, really? Like what?"

"Let's see, here," said Adair, squinting at the pages. "How about a bubble?"

Maude furrowed her eyebrows, then raised them. "A bubble? Are you insane?"

"No, I'm not. It's perfect!"

"How do you figure that?"

"Because, if we turn this old closet into a bubble, we can pop it! Then, we'll be free!" Adair exclaimed.

Maude looked at him, "Adair, that's the most brilliant idea you've ever come up with."

"Thanks. Now, let's get to work," he said, rising to his feet and handing Maude her wand. "Shine the light on this book, so I can see the spell."

"Sorry," Maude adjusted the light towards the page.

"Okay, here goes nothing," Adair took a breath. "Bubblunious Turnakas!"

Maude swished her wand at the door, and it slowly became see-through and a light pink color. The two friends looked down and saw that they could see the dirty floor below them, and the clothes and books around them began to slide to their feet in the round form that was taking shape.

"This is amazing!" Maude shouted, smiling at the view of Sini and Evel's room.

Suddenly they began to rise from the floor, and Adair looked uneasily at Maude.

"We have to pop it, quickly! Otherwise, we'll keep floating to the ceiling!"

He dropped the book and grabbed his wand.

"You ready?" Maude asked.

"Yeah," he replied, wand at the ready, pointing to the thin bubble layer in front of them.

"One...Two...Three...Go!" Maude commanded, as they both thrust their pointy wands forward and a big popping noise exploded across the room.

Adair and Maude tumbled to the floor, with shoes and clothes landing on top of them. They grunted and pushed up through Sini and Evel's belongings, trying to get out of the clutter.

"That was great! I'll have to remember that one," Adair smiled, brushing himself off.

"Yeah, that's a story for my parents, alright," Maude agreed, wiping off her robes.

"Now, what?" asked Adair, his eyes floating to the potion on the table.

"Forget that cauldron, Adair. We need to find the Head Mistress. She'll know how to properly dispose of it. Plus, I don't want to go near that stuff."

"It won't work unless there's a spell to help it," he added.

"I don't care. Come on," Maude grabbed the advanced spell book from the rubble and began to run out of the room, with Adair in tow.

The Head Mistress would receive them gratefully, for she was in some trouble of her own.

THE HEAD MISTRESS'S STUDY

Maude and Adair dashed to the Mistress's rooms, tripping over their robes and breathing heavily. When they arrived, they did not knock, but burst in and tripped over the little green man, who was cowering by the door.

"Oh, sir. We're sorry. What are you doing?" Maude exhaled.

"Don't go in there, children. It's not pretty," he stammered.

"What's going on?" Adair asked him, as he picked himself up off of the floor.

"The society is in there with her."

Maude's eyes widened and she looked to Adair. "It's begun. We have to stop it."

"Come on," Adair said, whipping out his wand.

The two friends tiptoed around the corner and down to the Head Mistress's study. They peeked around the doorway, and, sure enough, the children of the society members had wands extended and were circled around the Head Mistress. She seemed to have no wand, and her face was full of worry.

Maude pulled her head out of sight again, "Adair, what's the spell for getting the wands out of their hands?"

"How should I know? You're the one with the advanced spell book in your hand," he whispered back.

"Oh, I forgot," she swallowed and began flipping through the book for the spell.

Adair leaned around the corner and looked at the Head Mistress, "Hurry, Maude. This could get ugly."

"Okay, I found it. But, I'm going to throw them off, first. Then, once we get in there, I'll see what we need to do," she tossed the book to the ground and pulled out her wand.

"Whatever you think is best," Adair looked worried.

"Drop your wands!" Maude bellowed to the society, coming around the corner.

The eyes of sixteen adults and Sini, Evel, and a few other students turned to look at her.

Sini grinned, "Pay no attention to the little snoop. She's a complete idiot and has been trying to ruin this plan from the beginning."

"She's not an idiot!" Adair screamed, as he jumped out, wand in hand. "She's a lot better than you, Sini. She cares about this school! You don't!"

"She only cares about what it can do for her. She needs to learn all she can, or she'll never make it," Evel snapped.

"Wandly Flionous!" Maude cried, as the wands flew out of all the wicked children's hands. The sticks floated in the air ten feet above them, and their surprised faces turned to glares, as they focused back to Maude.

"Idiot, am I?" Maude grinned.

"Look, little girl. You think you know everything?" Sini's father growled, pushing through the students.

"Groundito Floponous!" Sini shouted, after pulling another wand from her robes.

Maude flew across the room and landed on the floor, a crumpled, groaning heap. She shook her head, trying to see straight, but the society was all a blur.

Sini grinned at her father, "You can never have enough wands on hand."

The society focused back on Mistress Avalon, as Sini came up to her with her wand extended.

"Now, Head Mistress, we can make this easy or difficult, if you'd like. Turn this school over to us. There are many more of us who have not arrived yet. I am sure you will be outnumbered, if this is all you can come up with," Sini's dad motioned to Adair, looking shocked, and Maude, crouched on the floor.

"These two students care about their school. It is not to be used for evil. I trusted you!" the Mistress yelled to the group.

"And, right you should. We are working for the better of our world. Crush our plans, and our world becomes an unhappy place. We don't want that do we?" he snarled, and the rest of the society cackled.

"We will not stand here and have our school's students be destroyed. For, in doing this, you hurt some of your own children!" Adair shouted to them.

"Not hurt, just diminish their powers," the man argued.

"They're too young to use them anyway," a woman in the circle added.

"No, we're not! You're just reaching for any possible way to make yourselves feel better about what you're doing!"

"Not so," another man, in a gray cloak, said. "We know exactly what we're doing and why. Do you actually think we rushed into this, young man? It took years of thought and decision making."

"Well, those years didn't pay off," Maude said, pulling herself from the floor. "We won't let you."

She swished her wand and pointed it at Sini's father, who began to laugh.

"Young lady...," he began.

"Her name is Maude," Evel sneered.

"Alright, Maude. Do you actually think that, just because you know all about us, you can stop this plan? You forget that we know more and are stronger than you."

"Oh, yeah?" Adair puffed up.

"But, you forget, sir," Maude seethed, gripping her courage charm around her neck with her free hand and praying for some of that power. "We have power and you don't."

"You forget, as well, that we have this," and he pulled out a small vile of the bubbling neon pink potion. "And, I think we shall begin with you."

THE WIZARD GOVERNMENT

Maude cowered, backing away from the potion, with wide eyes. Adair looked at Sini and her father closing in on his friend. He rushed over to Maude and jumped in front of her.

"Not if I have anything to do with it," he growled at Sini.

With piercing eyes, Sini glared at him, "Move back, kid. You don't want it done to you first, do you?"

Adair tumbled to the side, sorry to abandon Maude, but he feared Sini's evil glare. At that moment, Adair discovered he really was a coward, even when it came to saving the powers of his best friend.

"Adair?" she whimpered. "What do we do?"

He could only whisper, upset with his lack of courage, as he stood by her, "I don't know what to do, Maude." All he could do was grab her hand and face whatever happened, by her side. She smiled at him, as he squeezed her small hand, and then turned back with a glare to the evil society.

"Let's see. This is a momentous occasion," Sini's father beamed to his fellow society mates, as Sini kept her wand on Maude. "Does anyone have anything to say?"

He looked to the Head Mistress, who was backed against her desk by the few children surrounding her, who had just whipped out extra wands from their robes.

"Head Mistress, you don't seem to be taking charge of this school, as you should. You might have suspected this all along. Now, look where we are. Pointing wands at the most distinguished witch of our world. Pretty soon, she will be powerless. Isn't that a shame? Then, you will lose your precious school," he snarled.

Maude and the Mistress looked at each other, and the younger witch raised her eyebrows, as if questioning their next move. Maude wondered where all of Mistress Avalon's power was and why she didn't have other wizards there to fight with them. After all, she was one of the most powerful and accomplished in their world. Where was her wand? Why wasn't she saving them?

"I will not lose my school," Mistress Avalon said, her chin raised in defiance.

Sini's father looked back at her, "And, why not? Lose all your power, lose all of your students."

"She won't lose us," Maude added.

"Yeah," Adair agreed.

"We'll just see about that," Sini said, putting her wand to Maude's head. "Come on, Dad. I've been waiting for this for a while, now. Let's get on with it."

Maude winced at the wand's pressure on her temple, and Adair stood in shock and fear, trembling so hard that his pants were shaking.

Sini's father turned his focus to Maude, with a nasty grin.

"Yes, let us begin," he stated.

Just then, a loud "Wandly Flionous!" was shouted across the room. Sini and her father glanced over to see all the teachers huddled in the doorway. Sini's second wand flew out of her hand, as did the others', and joined the previous wands in the air, floating above their heads.

Maude exhaled and grinned happily to see Professor Flight, Mr. Pondweed, Miss Monkeystrap, Professor Whiskflisk, and Mr. Willowbeans. Their eyes were dark and glared at the group of evil wizards, and they were clad in robes of deep purple, the color of the first year students.

"Thank goodness," Adair breathed, as the teachers slowly entered the doorway.

"Oh, good evening, Professors," Sini's father bowed.

"Don't think we're blind to your little scheme, Mont. We know all about it, and weren't going to take this lying down," said Mr. Flight, waving his wand at Sini and her father to back away from Maude.

"How did all of you find out?" Mont wondered.

"The Head Mistress, of course," Mr. Pondweed added.

Mont whirled on the Mistress, "You knew about this before tonight? How?"

"I told her," Maude glared at him.

"You said that you could keep her quiet, Evel," Mont turned to the young witch, who cowered in his large shadow.

"I thought she had been quiet about it, sir," Evel told Sini's father.

"Well, obviously, she wasn't," he roared.

"Now, you're in bigger trouble than you imagined," Miss Monkeystrap said.

Into the doorway came a tall man, sturdy and strong, in beaming robes of white. He had a stern face, and his eyes flashed at the powerless wizards, who looked shocked at his appearance. His long blonde hair shone, and his black eyes darted from one society member to the next. He carried his golden wand outstretched and at the ready, and behind him trailed ten men in silver robes. Their robes had a black emblem on the chest, "WG," and Maude thought maybe they were the Wizard Government. She had never seen them in person, and this shining group seemed to have control of everyone in the room. The wizards in the silver robes lined up on either side of the wizard in white, and they looked menacingly at the cowering society.

"Who is that?" Adair whispered to Maude.

"I have no idea," she replied, staring at the man, whose presence seemed to take up the whole room.

"Mont, Mont, Mont...," the man shook his head. "Why must I be called here to the castle at this hour?"

"Oh, Head Wizard, sir." Mont Ster stumbled over his words. "Didn't expect to see you."

"The Secret Prison awaits you. You and your society. You have disgraced our government and our craft," he said, while turning to the evil young students. "But, these children. Why did you involve the children?" The Head Wizard looked at Sini, Evel, and their friends, who now stood helpless.

"I...well, sir....I...needed help in the school, and I....ummm...," Mont stammered.

"Now, these children must be shipped away, retire their wands, and face punishment from the Wizard Government. You took your next generation from learning and succeeding. Sad it all is. Take them from my sight," he sentenced them, with no chance to defend themselves. Maude sensed he already knew they all were guilty and knew the harshness they wanted to bring upon all of the students.

The men in silver robes waved their wands and the society was bounded, hands behind their backs. Sini and Evel struggled to be free and glared at Maude. Mont pleaded with the Head Wizard, as he stumbled after the tall man, groveling for mercy. Two of the men in silver grabbed Mont and held him back, so the Head Wizard could talk to Mistress Avalon in peace. Sini's dad whirled around and furrowed his eyebrows at Maude and the Head Mistress.

As they were being taken from the room, Sini leaned towards Maude, "You haven't seen the last of me yet, Maude Sinks! This is all your fault! You'd better watch out!"

Evel added, "Yeah, Maude! You could have been on our side! This crummy school won't teach you a thing!"

Maude sighed, as all of the evil presence was finally taken from the room, and she ran over to the Head Mistress.

"Are you alright? Sorry that we didn't get here sooner. We were kind of locked up for a little while," Maude explained.

The Mistress looked at Maude in shock and amusement, "You saved the school, Miss Sinks."

Maude stared back up at her, "I did?"

"You certainly did," Mistress Avalon smiled, as wands began dropping from the ceiling.

THE AWARD

"But, Mistress Avalon, as soon as I heard their plan, I did what any other student would do," Maude said, innocently.

"You went above and beyond, Maude. The plan was stopped because of you," Adair beamed, slipping his arm around his friend's shoulder.

"That's right, Mr. Tiptoe. She saved the school and kept all of our powers safe," the Head Mistress added.

"This calls for a celebration," the Head Wizard proclaimed. "All students will report to the dining hall tonight. And, you, young lady, will be our guest of honor."

The Head Wizard shook Maude's hand, and she smiled, brightly.

"Wow, really?" Maude turned to see Adair's disappointed face. "Sir, my friend here helped, also. He was with me the whole time. Can he be a guest of honor, too?"

"Of course! This will be the grandest feast this school has ever had, and your places will be at the head table with all of your teachers," he replied.

Adair and Maude hugged each other, happy to still have their powers and glad that their work paid off.

The Head Mistress shook hands with the Head Wizard, each smiling upon the children.

"Adair, you'd better go wash and change. You look a mess," Maude giggled.

"Oh, shut up, Maude," Adair smiled. "And, thanks."

The Head Wizard walked with Adair from the room, along with the Professors, who were congratulating the boy and tousling his hair. Maude was left alone with the Head Mistress.

"Mistress Avalon?" Maude began.

"What is it, dear?"

"I just wanted to thank you for believing in me. I was sure you would think I was crazy and made the whole thing up. I only wanted everyone in the school to be safe."

"I know, and you have succeeded."

Maude looked down, "But, I'm scared that I'll make a fool of myself at this celebration tonight."

"Why would you say that?" the Mistress asked.

"Well, I'm not such a good witch, after all. I'm clumsy and behind in all my subjects. I don't fit in. I don't know, maybe I should just sit at my regular table for the feast," Maude sighed.

"Nonsense," the woman said. "Maude, sit down a moment."

She obediently dropped into one of the chairs, as the Head Mistress sat at her desk, which was in shambles.

"Do you know that I was just like you?" she told Maude.

"What?"

"I was clumsy in school and didn't have many friends. When I was studying here, the time couldn't go fast enough. But, look what I became? I worked hard and my spell knowledge grew. After years of work, I became Head Mistress. You don't think I was born this way, do you?"

Maude's jaw hung open, as she stared in disbelief, "Do you mean that, one day, I could be a successful witch like you?"

"If you try hard enough, anything is possible. I worked to get where I am. Now, I have the respect of everyone in our world."

"Wow," Maude said. "You must never have had any fun. Studying all night is torture."

"Yes, but worth it. Trust me, dear. You will be fine. If you can get through something like this, you are a very special young witch. Believe in yourself, Maude."

Maude walked away, from her talk with Mistress Avalon, with her head held high and a new happiness and confidence. Sini was gone. Evel was gone. The wicked society was no more. She had beaten them. Maude Sinks had sunk their battleship. She grinned, as she walked to her room to dress, thinking of how, just maybe, she would walk through these halls, some day, as Head Mistress.

✳ ✳ ✳

That night, Maude washed and dressed in her best deep purple robes, and then she fluffed and primped her hair. She was just about to put the finishing touches on her cheeks with Rosy Rouge, when a knock came at her door. Maude opened it and found that no one was there. Her eyes flew up and down the hallway, but no one appeared. As she began to close the door, her glance fell on a package sitting on the floor. She looked again through the hall, but the deliverer seemed to have vanished.

Maude picked up the parcel, and read the tag. "TO THE BEST WITCH I KNOW, SIGNED YOUR FRIEND AND FELLOW SCREW-UP." She grinned and closed the door, excited to open the package. No one had ever sent her a parcel at school, except for her family. She knew it was from Adair and smiled at his thoughtfulness.

The young girl flopped on her bed and began to tear at the wrappings. As the paper fell from the box, Maude opened the parcel to find a dingy, old bottle. She looked confused until she saw the sticker on the side of the glass container. "Pure Toad Liver Oil, for hair brightening and delightful sparkle." Maude clasped the bottle in her hand and fell back on her bed, grinning ear to ear. She had definitely been wrong about Adair in the beginning of the school year, and she regretted thinking any ill thoughts of him, ever. He was her best friend, confidant, and true fellow screw-up. Although, their screw-ups had led them to save their friends and teachers from total ruin. Maude was glad Adair had been confident enough in her and in their plan. She had never felt better.

As Maude walked down the hall towards the dining room, her hair glistened brightly in the candlelight. She held her head high, tossed her long hair back, and adjusted her hat before entering the room. As she crossed into the doorway, she stopped, astounded that the entire school and all the teachers were already assembled. Their faces all were turned to her, and the teachers seemed to beam with pride. Maude gulped and began to walk to the front of the room, and the whole school burst into thunderous applause. Her face turned a bright red, as she took her place next to Adair, who was grinning and applauding like everyone else. He must have had the same welcome, because all the teachers at the table were patting the two young wizards' heads and nodding at them in congratulations.

"Hi, Adair," Maude said, happily. "Thanks for the gift."

"No problem. I figured it was your night to shine. I'm lucky to be seated by you, tonight," Adair admitted, his cheeks shading light pink.

"We did this together. Don't forget that," Maude reminded him, proudly.

"Yeah, but you started it. Without you, we never could have done it," he added.

Maude smiled brightly back at her friend, "But, I couldn't have done it without you."

The dining hall's applause died down, and the Head Mistress rose from her table, hands in the air.

"This is to be the grandest celebration our school has ever seen. This came to pass because of the daring minds and actions of Miss Maude Sinks and Mr. Adair Tiptoe. Their bravery saved our school and all of our powers. This is for them!" Mistress Avalon shouted and waved her wand, briskly, to each table as multiple plates and serving trays appeared with a wizard's delight. Maude practically shrieked at all of her favorite dishes appearing on the table. There were trays of BoogerBuns, Bat Whallops, Corn Collies, Dreadful Desserts, Malfunctioning Mouthfuls, many delicious cakes and cookies, and of course, goblets of her favorite drink, Snake Bite Juice. Adair grinned and began to dig in, as the rest of the hall finished gasping and clapping.

Maude was too excited to eat, so she only nibbled a bit on her BoogerBun. The Head Mistress looked over at her and smiled. That smile calmed Maude's thoughts and gave her a safe and comfortable feeling. No one, except for Adair, had fully believed in her before. It was a new feeling. She was tangled in nerves and felt, since the whole school knew of their feats, that now she had a reputation to live up to. Her usual clumsiness would not prove her ability, and she still worried about passing her classes. But, Maude tried to push these thoughts from her mind, as she took a sip from her goblet and smiled back at the Head Mistress. The woman nodded, as if she understood Maude's concerns, and maybe she did.

As the feast came to an end and all the students sat back full and content, the Head Wizard rose from his place by the Head Mistress and raised his arms for attention. The students focused on him, and Maude shifted in her seat, anxious to hear his words.

"Students and teachers, alike, this has indeed been a joyous occasion. I take great pride in the strength of this school, and these two young first years have proven my faith correct. Now, I would like to award them. Come, sir, with the packages," and he motioned to the green man in the back of the room.

Maude looked to Adair, as the small man walked through the hall and approached the head table. He was carrying a large box in each hand, and he bowed, as he set them before the Head Wizard.

"Not many wizards receive these until graduation, but I have delight in presenting these two amazing students with these," the Head Wizard declared, and motioning Maude and Adair to stand, he handed them each one of the parcels.

Adair grinned and began to open his, as Maude nodded to the Head Wizard in appreciation. Maude opened her box to find the same as Adair. They were each presented with kittens. The young black cats writhed in their new owners' hands, and the room broke into another round of applause. Maude looked down at her new pet, and noticed that it was perfectly black, except for a small white dot under its chin. Adair's was smooth and completely black, and he held and kissed his little one.

Maude looked back at her kitten, "It's alright that you're not perfect. Neither am I." She hugged the warm kitten, soon to be named Misfit, close to her chest, promising to care for and love her little award.

THE WIZARD WALLOP

Maude's spring term began with a great deal of hope and desire to finish off the year well. She and Adair studied a lot together, taking occasional trips to Caspian to walk off their nerves about final exams and the writer's block for their end of the year papers. With all the worries about Sini behind her, Maude could concentrate much better, and her teachers saw her improvements, among the small, but still existent, stumbles.

One beautiful spring day, Adair asked her to play Wizard Wallop on the lawn. This game, made up by the two friends after their big fight with evil, had become quite popular amongst the first years. Turtain and Plaka always asked to join, if they saw a game coming together on the grasses of the school. Slowly, other students had come out to watch, and then after one game, asked to be a part of the next.

Wizard Wallop involved two sides of kids, each having a ball. They would throw the balls across the chalk-drawn line at the other team. If they hit someone, always below the belt, as was the rule, the thrower was able to whip out their wand and turn the person, who had been hit, into a animal. Toads seemed to be the most popular one chosen, and this slowed the other team down. It was actually quite amusing to the teachers, who would look on sometimes to see that nothing got out of hand, because the lawn would end up being littered with frogs, sheep, monkeys, rabbits, and giraffes. This was a funny sight to them, and the confused animals watched the balls being thrown around with great interest. Finally, only one young wizard would be left standing, his team announced the winner, and he would have to go around doing reversal spells to bring back his fellow dazed classmates, who reappeared on their hands and knees or in squatting positions.

Maude was happy to give up studying for the afternoon and glad to join in the game. She and Adair retrieved their balls from their dorms and headed outside, knocking on doors and asking people to come play. Plaka, Zoey, Turtain, and Margit followed them to the lawn, along with Mudge, Barter, Tristan, and Quinn, which were Adair's roommates, who had recently become big fans of Wizard Wallop. A few other students had shouted that they would change and be right out on the playing field, as soon as they could. Maude and Adair were, of course, team captains and began to pick teams, as other kids came running from the dorms and trickled out onto the lawn. Mr. Pondweed came to watch the activity, and Miss Monkeystrap decided to join him. The Head Mistress had heard the whooping and hollering of young voices, and she looked out of her window. Seeing other teachers there, she wandered down to the lawn to watch her two power savers battle each other in a friendly game.

Maude chose first, gaining Quinn, a strapping young wizard with a fine face and stern jaw. He was the strongest, and Adair groaned at losing him to her side. Adair chose Barter, and Maude then chose Turtain. This went back and forth, and finally when the teams were divided up, Maude went to her own side of the line with Quinn, Turtain, Mudge, Plaka, Ferd, Shen, and Brista. Adair began pumping up Barter,

Tristan, Zoey, Margit, Yonah, Mikal, and Lushad, telling them his ideas and what Maude's team's weak sides were.

Finally, when the teams were ready and had finished plotting their strategies, Maude and Adair walked to the line and shook hands, trying to be proper and professional. They stared each other down.

"Ready for my team, Miss Screw-up?" Adair snarled in fun.

"You bet, Mr. Screw-up," Maude grinned. "Let's go!"

Mr. Pondweed gladly whistled, and the game began. Maude threw the first ball, because Adair insisted that girls go first, and she whacked Zoey right in the leg. Her roommate looked up at her with a sad face, "Why am I always the first one to go?"

Maude smiled right back at her and tugged out her wand, "I don't know."

With that, she turned Zoey into a rabbit, for she reminded Maude of a cute, innocent bunny.

Adair grabbed his team's ball, determined to make Maude pay for that one, and threw it across missing Quinn by an inch. "Oh, man! That was so close!" he shrieked, watching Maude's ball whiz past his face. "Hey! You're throwing too high!"

"Sorry!" Mudge shouted back to him, being that his throws were never any good, and he moved too slowly.

The game went back and forth, and Miss Monkey-strap was practically in tears when Tristan turned Plaka into a fish by accident and then turned her into a rhino, quickly, so she could breathe. With team balls and spells flying through the air, the Head Mistress was having a delightful time.

"Who came up with this fabulous game?" she asked Mr. Pondweed.

"Why, Maude and Adair, of course. Didn't you know?" he beamed.

"I had no idea," she looked back to the children, watching Maude chuck a ball and Adair wipe sweat from his brow. "Maybe this should be a school game! We could make up teams from the best in each class. Wouldn't it be fun to watch the first years take on the eighth years?"

"That's a wonderful idea!" Miss Monkeystrap added, gleefully.

The teachers turned back to the game, determined not to miss something. Once the lawn had become a zoo and the only ones standing were Adair and Maude, they each held their team balls under their arms and wands in the other hand. They looked across the grass at each other's muddy faces and grinned.

"Looks like it's just you and me," Maude said, watching a turtle crawl over the chalk-line to her side.

"Yep, sure does," he said, determined not to be a monkey that day.

"Take your best shot," dared Maude, and Adair threw the ball, missing her ankle by a smidge, when she jumped out of the way. "Is that all you got?"

"See what you can do," Adair challenged, and Maude flung her ball at him, hitting him square in the knee and sending him backwards into the grass.

"Are you okay?" Maude began to race to him.

"Yeah," he sat up, a little dazed. "Can we just skip the part about me being a monkey, this time? Last game, it took you an hour to remember the reversal spell, and scratching myself and swinging from trees are not my best characteristics."

Maude laughed and held out her hand to help Adair up from the ground.

He looked at her with raised eyebrows, "I don't trust you."

"It's just a hand. My wand is over here," she told him.

"I don't believe you, Maude Sinks," he smirked.

"Well, have a nice flight, then," and she turned him into a parrot.

The purple parrot looked up at her, wide-eyed, and said, "Adair want a cracker!"

With that, Maude lost it and fell on the grass, laughing. The teachers roared on the side lines, and Mistress Avalon's eyes sparkled, as she had definitely found a new school game.

THE WIZARD FESTIVAL

That term, Maude managed to pass her classes by the skin of her teeth, applying herself and studying a great deal. Adair did well and passed with flying colors, which didn't surprise Maude. She knew he would do well.

As they lounged in the airy courtyard after finals, Maude breathed in the fresh air and felt a good deal of weight lifted from her shoulders. With their lessons complete for the year, she could return home and tell her parents with confidence that she had done well. The only thing left to finish their term was the yearly Wizard Festival. It happened that this festival was right around the time of the students' completion of their school work. Maude was excited to arrive at the festival, see her parents, and tell them about how she had not only done well in class, but also saved her powers from total ruin.

Adair and Maude collected all their books and clothes, placed them in boxes and trunks, and set them in the hall with all the other students' things. They were to return that night to retrieve them, once the festival was over. Maude dressed and got ready to see her parents, putting a great deal of the toad liver oil in her hair.

Maude walked with Adair across the lawn towards the town, Lebria, where the festival would take place, ending the day with the Bunson Beauties' winner and her float ride through the streets. Lebria was in the opposite direction from Caspian, over a few hills and through a few gullies. Once the two friends arrived, they chatted and walked about the festival booths with their classmates, marveling at the new brooms, bats, cauldrons, and oils being sold. Adair, of course, dragged Maude to all the stands selling food, and he stocked up on BoogerBuns, candies, and drinks. Maude wondered how any one wizard could eat as much as he did, but rather than lecturing, she smiled and munched along with him. She bought her father a tube of Hair Replacer, a spider ring for her mom, and for her brother, Mickey, a toy ball which held a scorpion inside. She shuddered at the live creature in the ball and stuffed the toy in her bag. Adair wandered around with her and purchased a set of warming mittens for his mother, a broom polishing kit for his father, and a bunch of toys for his siblings. The two children smiled at their presents and walked over to the information stand for their school.

Mr. Pondweed was sitting in the booth, and he smiled at the approaching kids.

"Well, if it isn't our little power savers," he beamed at them.

"Hi, Mr. Pondweed. How are you today?" Maude smiled back.

"Hi, sir," said Adair.

"Find anything interesting?" their teacher asked.

"Oh, yes," Maude replied. "My father helps with this festival every year. It just gets better and better."

"I didn't know your dad was on the council for this event. That must be nice. You must know all about it, before it even happens. The rest of us just have to wait to find out what the new booths will be and what we'll be seeing each year," Mr. Pondweed added.

"Yeah, but this year I knew nothing, being away from home and all. He wouldn't even write about it to me. I think he wanted it to be a surprise this time," she said.

"Oh, well, how nice," her teacher smiled.

"There you are!" Maude heard a familiar voice and turned to see her mother approaching, holding Mickey's hand, and her dad following behind them.

"Mom!" She ran into her mother's arms and was enveloped in that warmth she had loved all of her life.

"How have you been, Dad? The festival going well so far?" she smiled at her father, who looked like he needed a good nap.

"Fine, I guess. No arrests thus far, so that's good. Last year was dreadful," her dad yawned.

"We've heard that your year has been quite busy," her mom smiled at her, knowingly.

"You found out, already?" Maude was sad that she couldn't deliver the news about the society, herself.

"Of course. You didn't think the school would keep that a secret from your own parents, do you? We just received a letter from the Head Mistress. I think all the parents did, except those that were involved in that stupid society," her mother smiled.

"We're proud of you, dear. Never thought it possible," Maude's dad grinned and wrapped his arms around her.

"Thanks, Dad," Maude said, happily.

Adair cleared his throat, next to her.

"Oh, Adair. I'm sorry," Maude brought him up in front of her. "Mom, Dad, you remember Adair from down the street? He was with me through it all. Without him, I would have never helped the school."

Her parents shook Adair's hand politely, and Mickey looked up at him, wide-eyed, remembering his sister's new friend falling down a hill, at one time.

"Nice to see you again, Mr. and Mrs. Sinks," he smiled.

"Well, you both did an excellent job. Without you, our powers might not be here today," Mr. Pondweed put in.

Maude blushed at the compliments and heard the hawk screech to announce that the parade was beginning.

"We'd better head over to the parade. I need to be there and meet my other associates," her dad informed them.

"Come on, Mickey," Maude's mother grabbed his little hand, as he still stared at his sister's best friend.

Maude and Adair walked excitedly behind her parents to the street and waited in the crowd to see the magicians, wicked clowns, and the big final float of the Bunson Beauty Queen. Adair munched on some snacks, offering a few to Mickey, who took them happily. Maude shifted, as she watched the parade go down the street. Honestly, she would rather have been at the stands, looking at all the great items they were selling, than at the parade. She had secretly been hoping that maybe she and Adair would have ridden in the parade, due to their accomplishments at the school.

When the time came for the final float, the crowd of wizards shoved and pushed to get a good look at the young witch who had won the contest. Maude didn't care much for the contest, so she didn't strain to see the girl's face. Instead, she reached into her pocket for her packet of Piercing Popcorn, when Adair gasped and grabbed Maude's arm, spilling her corn.

"What is it, Adair?"

"It's Evel!" Adair yelped.

"What?!" Maude answered, straining her neck to see the float.

Sure enough, sparkly hair and all, Evel sat on the large throne atop the final parade float. She grinned wickedly and waved to the applauding crowd of wizards surrounding the street. Maude looked to Adair, in shock, and saw that he had the same speechless expression.

"Just how did she do that?" Maude hissed. "They were taken away! We watched Evel and Sini be led away by those men in silver cloaks! What happened?"

"I have no idea," breathed Adair, still looking, open mouthed, at the float.

"Dad! You have to fix this!" Maude shrieked, pulling at her father's robes.

"Fix what?" he asked, confused by his daughter's yelling.

"That's Evel up there! The one I wrote to you about! You said we were too young to enter! How can she be the winner? She was just arrested for trying to take over the school!" Maude explained in breaths of fury.

"The only way she could be in the parade is if she won the contest. No foul play is allowed. Don't worry, dear. I'll get to the bottom of this," her father assured her, and left them, pushing through the crowd to find his associates.

Maude whirled to face Adair, who still stood there staring in disbelief.

"This is crazy, Maude," he whispered to her. "Something must have happened. Maybe she escaped. Where is the *REAL* winner?"

"She would do anything to be up there, Adair, and we know that. We have to find out what's going on."

Maude grabbed her friend's arm and headed through the people, towards the street, to get a closer look. When the float had passed and the crowd seemed pleased and was dwindling, Maude stared after the pretend Bunson Beauty winner. A small stone lifted from the end of the float, and Sini's head popped up. Maude and Adair gasped and held onto each other, as the girl glared at them, wickedly. Her evil smile caused those familiar shivers to slide down Maude's spine, and she turned to Adair, "They escaped! Both of them! We have to do something! They'll come after the school, again."

"We don't have to worry, now. School is over, re- member? We just have to tell the Head Mistress that they are on the loose again," Adair whined. He had hoped that all of this insanity was over.

"But, what about next term?" Maude looked at Adair and then back to the float. Sini glared at them, waved evilly, and disappeared under the stone trap door. Maude heaved a sigh, as her head spun with realizations that the summer would not be much of a vacation. She would have to watch her back at all times.

Adair looked at his concerned friend, "Maude, there's nothing we can do, until they act again. Hope- fully, the society is being tried by the Wizard Govern- ment, and then Sini and Evel are in this by them- selves."

"Yeah," Maude agreed. "That's what worries me."

✳ ABOUT THE AUTHOR ✳

Becky Titelman has been writing her whole life, from pasting papers together and using stickers for the pictures, to writing a full length story from the ages of nine to thirteen. At twenty-six, she is thrilled to finally see her newest work in print. Being a professional singer, dancer, and actress at heart, Becky decided to take a little time off from auditioning to concentrate on her other love, writing. Originally from Forest Hill, Maryland, she now resides in New York City, living with her favorite Weimeraner, Nimbus.

Printed in the United States
46884LVS00001B/28-156

9 781420 859119